THE ADVENTURES OF TOM SAWYER

The *Oxford Progressive English Readers* series provides a wide range of reading for learners of English.

Each book in the series has been written to follow the strict guidelines of a syllabus, wordlist and structure list. The texts are graded according to these guidelines; Grade 1 at a 1,400 word level, Grade 2 at a 2,100 word level, Grade 3 at a 3,100 word level, Grade 4 at a 3,700 word level and Grade 5 at a 5,000 word level.

The latest methods of text analysis, using specially designed software, ensure that readability is carefully controlled at every level. Any new words which are vital to the mood and style of the story are explained within the text, and reoccur throughout for maximum reinforcement. New language items are also clarified by attractive illustrations.

Each book has a short section containing carefully graded exercises and controlled activities, which test both global and specific understanding.

The Adventures of Tom Sawyer

Mark Twain

Hong Kong
Oxford University Press
Oxford Singapore Tokyo

Oxford University Press

Oxford   New York   Toronto
Kuala Lumpur   Singapore   Hong Kong   Tokyo
Delhi   Bombay   Calcutta   Madras   Karachi
Nairobi   Dar es Salaam   Cape Town
Melbourne   Auckland   Madrid

and associated companies in
Berlin   Ibadan

Oxford is a trade mark of Oxford University Press

First published 1992
Third impression 1993

© Oxford University Press 1992

Illustrated by K.Y. Chan

Syllabus designer: David Foulds

Text processing and analysis by Luxfield Consultants Ltd.

ISBN 0 19 585333 4

Printed in Hong Kong
Published by Oxford University Press (Hong Kong) Ltd
18/F Warwick House, Tong Chong Street, Quarry Bay, Hong Kong

CURR
P2
7
.CSP4
Adu
1993

CONTENTS

1

BAD TOM

Tom must be punished

'Tom,' shouted Aunt Polly.

There was no answer.

'Tom,' she called again, but there was still no reply.

'Where is that boy? Tom!' and she shouted louder 5
than before.

She took off her glasses and looked around the room.
Then she stood up and went to the open door. She
looked out over the garden. No Tom.

'Y-o-u Tom!' 10

There was a noise behind her, and she turned round
quickly. She was just in time to catch hold of a small
boy by the back of his trousers.

'I had forgotten that
cupboard,' she said.
'What have you been
doing in there?'

'Nothing.'

'Nothing? Just look at
your hands and mouth.
What is that mess?'

'I don't know, Aunt.'

'Well, I know. It's jam,
that's what it is. You've
been in that cupboard
eating jam. I've told
you so many times to
leave that jam alone.
Give me that stick.'

The stick was held up high. Tom really was in trouble.

'Oh, look behind you, Aunt!' shouted Tom.

The old lady turned round to see what was the matter. This gave Tom time to jump up. He had climbed over the high wooden fence and was out of sight before his aunt knew what was happening.

Aunt Polly stood surprised for a minute. Then she began to laugh.

'Oh, that boy,' she said to herself. 'He's played so many tricks on me like that. I should have been ready for him. He'll stay away from school this afternoon, I know, so I'll have to make him work tomorrow, to punish him. It's very hard to make him work on Saturdays, when all his friends are having a holiday. He hates work more than anything else, but I shall have to punish him somehow.'

The fight

Tom walked down the street practising a new way to whistle. It made a very good sound, and he had only just learned how to do it.

Suddenly he stopped whistling. In front of him stood a boy, a little taller than himself. Tom had never seen him before.

The village of St Petersburg, where Tom lived with Aunt Polly, his brother Sid, and Mary, his sister, was a small, quiet place. You did not often see new people there. This boy was well-dressed, too. It was not Sunday, and he was well-dressed, which was very unusual. He even wore a tie. Tom stared at him, and the longer he stared, the dirtier his own clothes seemed. Neither boy spoke. If one moved, the other moved, sideways. They circled around one another, face to face, eye to eye all the time.

At last Tom spoke.

'I can beat you.'

'I'd like to see you try it.'

'Well, I can.'

'No, you can't.'

'Yes, I can.'

'No, you can't.'

'I can.'

'You can't.'

'Can.'

'Can't.'

There was an uncomfortable silence. Then Tom said, 'What's your name?'

'It isn't your business.'

'Well, I'll make it my business.'

'Well, why don't you?'

'If you say much more I will.'

'Much more, much more, much more. There, now.'

'Oh, you think you're very clever, don't you? I could beat you with one hand tied behind my back, if I wanted to.'

'Well, why don't you do it? You say you can do it.'

'Well, I will if you don't watch out.'

'Well, go on then. Why do you keep talking about it? Why do you keep saying you will? It's because you're afraid.'

'I'm not afraid.'

'You are.'

'I'm not.'

'You are.'

There was another silence, and more staring at each other and moving round. Soon they were shoulder to shoulder.

Tom said, 'Get away from here.'

'Get away yourself.'

'I won't.'

'I won't either.'

So they stood there, pushing at each other as hard as they could. In another minute they were rolling in the dirt. They pulled and tore at each other's hair and clothes. They scratched each other's noses, and covered themselves with dust. Tom at last got on top of the new boy, sat on him and hit him with his fists.

'Say enough,' he said.

The boy only tried harder to get free. He was very angry, and his anger made him cry.

'Say enough,' said Tom again, still hitting him.

At last the stranger managed to whisper, 'Enough,' and Tom let him get up.

'Now that will teach you,' he said. 'You'd better remember who you're talking to next time.'

Tom got home quite late that night. He climbed quietly in through the bedroom window. He did not want to wake his brother Sid, who shared his room, or Aunt Polly, who slept downstairs. But Aunt Polly was awake, waiting for him. She was very angry when she saw the mess his clothes were in. She promised herself that she would make Tom's Saturday into a day of hard work.

Hard work

On Saturday morning Tom appeared outside his house. He was carrying a bucket of paint and a brush with a long handle. He looked at the fence and took a deep breath. The fence was thirty yards long and nine feet high. His punishment was to paint it.

It seemed to him that there was no joy in the world. He sighed as he dipped his brush in the paint and passed it along the top board. He did it again, and then stood back. He looked at the tiny piece he had painted and then at the rest of the fence, still to be done. It was too much.

Just then Jim came running out of the house carrying a bucket. Jim was a small boy who worked for Aunt Polly. He was going to the town well to get water.

Tom had always hated that job, but now it seemed to him the best job in the world. There were always boys and girls at the well, waiting for their turn. Tom remembered that it always took Jim an hour or more to go and get the water.

'Jim,' he called, 'I'll go and get the water if you will paint some fence for me.'

Jim shook his head.

'Can't do that, Tom. Your aunt would beat me if she found out.'

'She wouldn't beat you, Jim. She never beats anybody. She talks an awful lot, but talk doesn't hurt. I'll give you a marble if you'll do it.'

Tom showed him the little ball of coloured glass. Jim began to look interested.

'It's a white one, Jim.'

White marbles were hard to get. Jim put down his bucket and took the marble. But in another minute the scene changed. Jim was running down the road with his bucket and a sore bottom. Tom was painting very hard, and Aunt Polly was going back into the house with a slipper in her hand.

Tom's new interest in painting did not last for long. He began to think of the fun he had planned for this day, and he felt worse than ever. Soon the other boys would come along, and they would laugh at him for having to work. The thought of that burnt him like fire.

Suddenly he had a wonderful idea. He took up his brush and started to work.

Ben Rogers came along the road, eating an apple. He stopped to watch.

Tom went on painting. He paid no attention to Ben. He stood back to look at his work, as an artist might look at a beautiful painting. Then he painted the top of the next board, and stood back to look at it again.

Ben came and stood beside him. Tom's mouth watered for the apple, but he kept on working.

'Hello,' said Ben at last, 'have you got to work?'

'Oh, it's you Ben, I didn't see you there,' replied Tom.

'I'm going swimming. Don't you wish you could? But of course you'd rather work, wouldn't you?'

'What do you call work?' answered Tom, looking at him.

'Isn't that work?'

Tom continued his painting, and answered carelessly, 'Well, perhaps it is, and perhaps it isn't. All I know is, it is all right for Tom Sawyer.'

'You don't mean to say you like doing it?'

The brush continued to move.

'Like it? Well, I don't see why I shouldn't like it. Does a boy get a chance to paint a fence every day?' Ben stopped eating his apple. Tom moved his brush along the fence. He stepped back, then added a bit more paint here and there. Ben was watching every move. He was getting more and more interested. Then he said, 'Tom, let me paint a little.'

The helpers

Tom looked as if he was about to say yes, then changed his mind.

'No, no, Ben, I don't think I should. You see, Aunt Polly is very hard to please. This fence is at the front of the house, you see. If it was the back fence I wouldn't mind. But this one has got to be done very carefully. I don't suppose there is one boy in a thousand, maybe two thousand, that can do this the way it's got to be done.'

'Is that right?' said Ben in surprise. 'Oh, come now, let me just try, only just a little. I'd let you if you were me, Tom.'

'Ben, I'd like to, really I would, but if you were to paint this fence and anything went wrong with it, Aunt Polly would be so angry. Jim wanted to do it and she wouldn't let him. Sid wanted to do it, and she wouldn't let Sid either.'

'Oh, come on. I'll be careful. Now just let me try and I'll give you some of my apple.'

'But Aunt Polly, Ben,' said Tom.

'I'll give you all of the apple.'

Tom gave up the brush. And while Ben worked in the sun, Tom sat in the shade eating the apple. He planned how he could trick the other boys into doing his work for him.

Boys came along the road every little while. They came to laugh, but stayed to paint. By the time Ben was tired out, Tom had given the next chance to Billy Fisher for a kite. And when he was tired Johnny Miller took his place, in exchange for a very interesting dead rat.

So it went on, hour after hour. And when the middle of the afternoon came, Tom had a pile of good things. He had, besides the things I have mentioned, twelve marbles, a piece of blue bottle-glass to look through, a key that wouldn't unlock anything, a piece of chalk, the glass top of a wine bottle, a toy soldier made of metal, two fish in a jam jar, a kitten with only one eye, a dog collar (but no dog), the handle of a knife and an old piece of rope. He had had a nice lazy time all the while, with plenty of people to talk to, and the fence had three coats of paint on it. If there had been enough paint, he would have taken things from every boy in the village.

Tom went to find Aunt Polly. She was sitting in the back room.

'May I go out and play now, Aunt?' he asked.

'What, already? How much have you done?'

'It's all done, Aunt.'

'Tom, don't lie to me, I don't like it.'

'I'm not lying, Aunt. It is all done.'

Aunt Polly did not believe him, so she went out to see. When she found the whole fence painted she was very surprised.

'So you can work when you feel like it, Tom,' she said. 'Now you can go and play.'

HUCKLEBERRY FINN

Tom enjoys church

The next day Tom had to go to Sunday school and the morning meeting in church. It was not a thing he usually liked doing. He hated having to get dressed in his best clothes. He spent most of the time in Sunday school pulling the girls' hair. The teacher had to tell him to behave himself more than once.

At half past ten all the children marched into church to sit with their parents. Tom never listened to the prayers or the speeches. He didn't sing any of the hymns. His mind was on other things. This morning he had brought a large black beetle to church with him. It was in a box in his pocket. During the priest's talk, which was so boring that many people were soon almost asleep, he took the box out and opened it.

Immediately the beetle pinched his finger with its sharp jaws. Tom shook his hand, and hurriedly put a sore finger into his mouth. The beetle was thrown onto the floor and lay on its back, unable to turn over. Tom looked at it and wanted to get it back, but it was too far away. Other people round Tom had noticed the beetle, and they were watching it too.

Someone had brought a little dog into the church. He came and looked at the beetle. He began to wag his tail excitedly. He walked all round it, and smelt it from a safe distance. Then he walked round it again, nearer this time. At last he got too clever, and touched it with his nose. There was a cry of pain as the dog shook his head, and the beetle fell two yards away on its back again.

Many people sitting near Tom had to hide their faces in their handkerchiefs to stop themselves laughing. The dog looked around and began to attack the beetle again, this time with his paws. He jumped at it several times, but when it did not move he got tired of the game. He followed an ant instead, but grew tired once more. He yawned, sighed, completely forgot about the beetle and sat down on it.

Then there was a wild scream of pain as the beetle pinched the dog, and held on to him. The dog raced up and down the church, yelping noisily. He ran past the priest and returned to his master, who quickly put him outside. The little dog's cries of pain faded away as he ran off into the distance.

By this time everybody in the church was red-faced with silent laughter. Although the priest continued with his boring talk about good and bad behaviour, no one was really listening.

When Tom went home he was quite cheerful. He had enjoyed his visit to church that morning. There was only one thing wrong. He thought it was all right for the dog to play with his beetle, but it was unkind of him to run away with it.

Tom's sore toe

On Monday morning Tom Sawyer was unhappy, because it was the start of another week in school. He lay in bed thinking. He wished he was sick, then he could stay at home. He felt himself all over, but could find nothing wrong. Suddenly he discovered something. One of his upper teeth was loose. This was lucky. He was just going to start making noises as if he were in pain, when he remembered something. If he complained about a bad tooth, his aunt would pull it out, and that would hurt. So he decided not to make that an excuse for staying at home. He felt himself all over again, and this time he found a sore toe. It wasn't really that bad, but Tom decided to use it as his excuse.

He lay in bed making horrible noises as if he was in great pain. Sid was fast asleep. Tom groaned even louder than before. Sid woke up and came over to Tom's bed.

'What's the matter, Tom?' he asked.

'Oh Sid, don't touch me,' groaned Tom.

'Why, what's the matter, Tom? I must call Auntie.'

'No, don't bother. It will all be over soon. Don't call anybody.'

'But I must. Don't groan like that, Tom, it's terrible.'

'I forgive you all the bad things you have ever done to me, Sid,' said Tom, still groaning.

'Oh, Tom. You're not dying, are you? Don't Tom, please don't die.'

'I forgive everybody, Sid. Tell them so, Sid.'

But Sid had gone. He ran downstairs and shouted.

'Oh, Aunt Polly, come quickly. Tom's dying.'

'Dying?'

'Yes. Don't wait, come quickly.'

'Don't be silly. I don't believe it.'

But she ran upstairs, with Sid and Mary close behind her.

When she got to Tom's bedside she said, 'Tom, what's the matter with you?'

'Oh, Auntie, it's my sore toe. It's dead.'

'Oh, Tom. What a fright you gave me. Now stop this noise, and get out of that bed.'

'Aunt Polly, it seemed dead, and it hurt so much that I even forgot about my sore tooth,' replied Tom.

'Your tooth, what's the matter with your tooth?'

'It's loose and it hurts.'

'Open your mouth and let me see,' said his aunt. 'Yes, you have got a loose one there, but you're not going to die because of that. Mary, get me a silk thread and a piece of coal from the kitchen fire.'

'Oh, please Auntie, don't pull it out. It doesn't hurt any more. Please don't, Auntie. I don't want to stay at home from school.'

'Oh, you don't, don't you? So all this noise was because you thought you'd be able to stay at home from school and go fishing. You are a bad boy, Tom.'

By this time Mary had returned. The old lady tied one end of the thread to Tom's tooth, and the other end to the bed-post. She took the piece of hot coal, and suddenly pushed it almost into the boy's face. Tom's head pulled back fast, and now the tooth was out, hanging on the thread by the bed-post.

Plans for an adventure

As Tom was on his way to school that morning he met Huckleberry Finn. Huck was the son of a man who was always drunk. He had no mother, and no-one looked after him. All the mothers of the town disliked him because he was lazy, wild, rude and bad. None of the children were allowed to play with him. Tom wished he could live like Huck, but, like the rest, he had been told not to play with him. So he played with him every time he got the chance.

Huckleberry was always dressed in old clothes that were far too big for him. He wore a dirty hat and nothing on his feet. He slept on doorsteps in fine weather, and in an empty barrel when it was wet. He did not have to go to school or to church, and he did not have to obey anybody. He could go fishing or swimming when he liked. Nobody told him not to fight. He could go to bed as late as he wished. He never had to wash or put on clean clothes. He was every boy's dream of what a boy should be.

'Hello, Huck,' said Tom.

'Hello yourself.'

'What have you got there?'

'A dead cat.'

'Let me see him, Huck. Oh, he's really stiff. Where did you get him?'

'I bought him from a boy.'

'What are dead cats good for, Huck?'

'Good for? They cure spots on your skin.'

'How can they do that, Huck?'

'Well, you take your cat and go to the graveyard about midnight. You have to find a place where someone who was wicked has been buried. When it's midnight a devil will come, or maybe two or three. You can't see them, you can only hear something like the wind. And while they're taking that wicked person away, you throw your cat after them and say, "Devil follow body, cat follow devil, spots follow cat, I'm finished with you". That will make any spots go away.'

'Did you ever try it, Huck?' asked Tom.

'No, but old Mother Hopkins told me about it.'

'Then I expect it's true. People say that she's a witch. When are you going to try the cat, Huck?'

'Tonight. I think the devils will come for Horse Williams tonight. He was buried two days ago, and he was wicked enough.'

'Let me go with you,' said Tom eagerly.

'Of course, if you're not afraid.'

'I'm not afraid. Will you make a noise like a cat under my window to let me know you're ready?'

'Yes, and you answer back if you get a chance. Last time I got bricks thrown at me for making a noise. You must be quicker this time.'

'I will, Huck. Last time I couldn't answer because Auntie was watching me, but I'll answer this time.'

So, with all plans made for the night's adventure, Tom continued on his way to school.

Tom's new friend

Tom was late for school. Although he tried to slip into his place without being noticed, the master caught him.

'Thomas Sawyer,' he called.

Tom knew that when his name was pronounced in full, it meant trouble.

'Sir,' he answered.

'Come here. Now, sir, why are you late again, as usual?'

Tom was going to tell a lie. Then he noticed that there was only one empty place on the girls' side of the classroom. That place was right next to someone he wanted to make friends with.

'I STOPPED TO TALK WITH HUCKLEBERRY FINN,' said Tom.

'You did what?' the master said, as if he could not believe what he had heard.

'I stopped to talk to Huckleberry Finn,' repeated Tom.

The master was so angry with Tom that he made him take off his jacket, and he gave him a good beating.

'Now, Mr Thomas Sawyer,' he said when he had finished with his stick, 'go and sit with the girls.'

All the children laughed at Tom as he took his place on the seat with the girls. Tom did not mind at all.

When he sat down, the girl moved away. She turned her back on him. Tom sat still and seemed to study his book. Soon, he began to look at the girl. She saw him looking, and made a face at him. He began drawing on his book, but kept his work hidden. For a while, the girl pretended not to notice, then she tried to see what he was doing. He still kept his hand over his work.

'Let me see it,' she whispered at last.

Tom took his hand away, It was a rather bad drawing of a house.

'It's nice,' she said. 'Make a man.'

Tom put a man in front of the house. He was much too big and could have stepped over the house, but the girl liked it.

'It's very nice,' she said. 'I wish I could draw.'

'I'll teach you, if you like,' whispered Tom.

'Oh, will you? When?'

'Do you go home for lunch?'

'I'll stay if you will.'

'Good. What's your name?'

'Becky Thatcher. What's yours? Oh, I know. It's Thomas Sawyer.'

'I'm only called that when I'm in trouble. I'm Tom when I'm good. You call me Tom, will you?'

'Yes.'

When school ended at lunch time, Tom gave Becky her drawing lesson. He liked this little girl, and made her promise to be his friend for ever.

3

THE GRAVEYARD

The devils are coming

At half past nine that night, Tom and Sid were sent to bed as usual. They said their prayers and Sid was soon asleep. Tom lay awake and waited. When it seemed to him that it must be nearly morning, he heard the clock strike ten. Oh, how slowly the time passed.

He lay still and looked up into the dark. Everything was very quiet. He could hardly keep himself awake. The clock struck eleven, but he did not hear it. And then a most terrible noise started. At once a window was opened, and a voice cried, 'Go away, you noisy cat.' An empty bottle crashed against the outside wall, and Tom was suddenly wide awake. A minute later he was dressed and out of the window. He crept along the roof, making a noise like a cat once or twice. Then he jumped on to the wood-shed, and from there to the ground. Huckleberry Finn was waiting with his dead cat.

The boys moved off and disappeared in the darkness. It took them just half an hour to get to the graveyard.

The graveyard was on a hill, about a mile and a half from the village. The wind blew through the trees, and Tom thought it sounded like the noise of ghosts complaining because they had been woken up. The boys did not talk very much, and soon found the new grave they were looking for. They hid behind some trees.

Then they waited quietly for what seemed a long time. Only the noise of an owl broke the silence. At last Tom felt he had to speak.

'Huck, do you believe the dead people like us to be here?' he whispered.

'I wish I knew,' replied Huckleberry. 'It's awfully quiet, isn't it?'

Suddenly Tom pulled Huck's arm.

'What is it, Tom?' The two boys held on to each other with fast beating hearts.

'Shh. There it is again. Didn't you hear it?'

'Oh, Tom, they're coming. What shall we do?'

'I don't know. Do you think they'll see us?'

'They can see in the dark the same as cats do. Oh, Tom, I wish I hadn't come.'

'Don't be afraid. I don't think they will bother us. If we keep still, maybe they won't notice us at all.'

'I'll try, Tom, but I can't stop shaking.'

The boys tried hard to see what was happening, and hardly breathed. The sound of voices came from the far end of the graveyard.

'Look there,' whispered Tom. 'What is it?'

'It's devil-fire. Tom, this is terrible.'

Some people came towards them out of the darkness. One was swinging an old lamp.

'It really is devils,' whispered Huck. 'Three of them. Can you pray, Tom?'

'I'll try, but don't be afraid. They aren't going to hurt us.' Tom began to say a prayer he knew.

'Shh.'

'What is it, Huck?'

'They're humans. One of them is, anyway. That's the voice of old Muff Potter.'

'No, that can't be true, can it?'

'I'm sure it is. Don't move. He won't see us. I expect he's drunk as usual.'

'All right, I'll keep still. Here they come. Huck, I know another of those voices. It's Injun Joe.'

A terrible sight

The three men had now reached the grave, and stood only a few feet from the boys' hiding place.

'Here it is,' said the third voice. The speaker held the lamp up high. The light shone on his face. It was young Doctor Robinson.

Potter and Injun Joe were pushing a cart with a rope and two spades on it. They put down their load and began to dig up the grave. The doctor put the lamp at the head of the grave, and came and sat down with his back against the tree. He was so close, the boys could have touched him.

'Hurry men,' he said in a low voice. 'The moon might come out at any moment.'

For some time there was no noise but the sound of the spades on the earth. Then a spade struck the coffin, and in another minute or two the men had pulled it up. They took off the lid, got out the body, and put it on the ground. The cart was made ready, and the body placed on it, covered with a blanket, and tied in place with the rope. The rope was too long so Potter took out a large knife and cut it. Then he said, 'Now, the body you wanted is all ready, Doctor. You must give us another five dollars, or here it stays.'

'That's right,' said Injun Joe.

'What do you mean?' said the doctor. 'You asked for your pay before you did the job, and I've paid you.'

'Yes,' said Injun Joe, 'but I want more than that. Five years ago you chased me away from your father's house   5
one night when I came to ask for something to eat. You said I was there to steal something. I promised myself I'd make you pay for doing that. Your father had me put in jail because of you. Did you think I'd forget? Now you've got to pay for it.'

He was shaking his fist in the doctor's face by this time. The doctor struck out suddenly and Injun Joe fell to the ground. Potter dropped his knife and shouted, 'Here, now. You can't hit my partner,' and the next minute he and the doctor were fighting. Injun Joe jumped to his feet. He picked up   25
Potter's knife, and crept round the two fighting men, looking for a chance to stick his knife into the doctor.

Suddenly the doctor got free. He lifted up a heavy board from the coffin, and hit Potter hard with it. Potter fell to the ground. At the same time, Injun Joe saw his   30
chance. He stuck the knife, up to the handle, in the young doctor's chest. The doctor fell on top of Potter, covering him with his blood. The clouds covered the moon, so that the two frightened boys could no longer see the terrible scene. They ran away in the dark.   35

A man lies dead

When the moon came out again, Injun Joe was standing over the two men. The doctor gave a long sigh and was still. Injun Joe robbed the doctor, and put the knife beside Potter's right hand. Then he sat down on the open coffin. Five minutes passed, and then Potter began to move. His hand closed on the knife. He lifted it up, looked at it, and let it fall. Then he sat up, pushing the doctor's dead body away from him. He looked at it for a minute, then looked around him. His eyes met Joe's.

'What happened, Joe?' he said.

'It's a dirty business,' said Joe.

'What did you do it for?'

'I didn't do it.'

Potter shivered and grew white.

'I shouldn't have had that drink tonight. I'm all mixed-up. I can't remember anything about it, really. Tell me, Joe, honestly, did I do it? I never meant to, Joe. Tell me how it happened. Oh, it's awful.'

'You two were fighting,' said Joe. 'He hit you with that piece of wood, and you fell flat. Then you got up, took the knife and stuck it in him, just as he hit you again. He fell on top of you.'

'Oh, I didn't know what I was doing. I never used a knife like that in my life before, Joe. I've fought, but never with a knife. Joe, don't tell. Say you won't tell. I always liked you, Joe. You won't tell, will you?' And the poor man dropped to his knees before the real murderer and took his hands.

'No, you've always been fair with me, Muff Potter. I won't say anything about it to anyone.'

'Oh, Joe, you're an angel from Heaven. I'll be thankful to you for ever for this,' and Potter began to cry.

'That's enough crying. This isn't the time for it,' said Joe. 'You go that way and I'll go this. Move now, and don't leave any tracks behind you.'

Potter started to run. The Indian stood looking after him.   5

'He's so drunk, he's forgotten the knife. He won't remember it till he's gone a long way. Then he'll be too afraid to come back and get it, the coward,' said Joe to himself.

Two or three minutes later the murdered man, the   20 body in the blanket, the empty coffin and the open grave were alone under the light of the moon.

Swearing in blood

The two boys ran on towards the village. They looked   25 back over their shoulders from time to time, as if they thought they might be followed. At last they reached an old, broken-down house. They ran in through the open door, and fell to the floor.

'What do you think will happen now, Huck?'   30 whispered Tom.

'If Doctor Robinson dies, I think someone will be hanged for it,' replied Huck.

'Do you really?'

'I know it, Tom.'   25

Tom thought for a minute, then he said, 'Who will tell? Shall we?'

'Of course not. If something happened, and Injun Joe isn't hanged, he'll kill us for knowing about it.'

'That's what I was thinking, Huck.'

'If anybody tells, let Muff Potter do it!'

5   Tom said nothing, but he was thinking. Soon he said, 'Huck, Muff Potter doesn't know about it. How can he tell?'

'Why doesn't he know, Tom? He was there, wasn't he?'

10   'Yes, Huck, but when Injun Joe stabbed the doctor with the knife, Muff Potter had been hit on the head and was lying on the ground.'

'That's right, Tom.'

'Do you think that bang on the head could have 15   killed him, too?'

'No, I don't think so. It wasn't hard enough for that.'

After another thoughtful silence, Tom said, 'Huck, are you sure you can keep quiet about all this?'

'Tom, we've *got* to keep quiet about it. Injun Joe will 20   be after us if he isn't hanged, and he won't care what he does to us. Let's swear to one another to keep quiet.'

'I agree, Huck. Shall we hold hands and swear?'

'Oh no, for a big thing like this, we've got to have writing and swear in blood.'

25   So they found a piece of wood, and with a red pencil that he found in his pocket Tom wrote these words:

>   *Huck Finn and Tom Sawyer swear they will keep quiet about this and they wish they may drop down dead and rot if they ever tell.*

30   Then they pricked their fingers and wrote the first letters of their names in blood. Tom had to help Huck for he could neither read nor write. They buried the wood close to the wall and promised not to speak of what they had seen again.

4

BAD DREAMS

Aunt Polly cries

Someone crept quietly in at the other end of the old
house now, but the boys did not notice. Suddenly a
dog started making a noise just outside. The boys held
on to each other, very afraid.   5

'If a dog howls like that it means something bad is
going to happen,' whispered Huck. 'Which way is he
looking?'

'I don't know. Look through that crack, quick.'

They looked out through a hole in the wall.   10

'The dog's got his back to us, Huck. He's not looking
at us.'

The howling stopped, but another sound came over
the night air.

'What's that?' whispered Tom.   15

'Sounds like pigs. No, it's somebody snoring, Tom.'

'That's right, Huck. Where is it coming from?'

'Sounds as if it's down the other end of the house.'

'Let's go and see,' said Tom.

'Do you think we should? It might be Injun Joe.'   20

Tom shivered. After a minute or two, the boys agreed
to go and see who it was, but to run if the snoring
stopped. So they went quietly, one behind the other.
When they got near to the snorer, Tom stepped on a
stick and it broke. The man moved a little and they   25
could see his face. It was Muff Potter.

The boys stood still. Their hearts seemed to stop
beating. Then the man turned over and he began to
snore again. Their fear passed. They went quietly out
of the house and stopped to talk. A long howl could   30

be heard again. They turned and saw the dog. He was looking towards Potter.

'The dog was howling at him, not us. Something awful will happen to him, you wait and see,' whispered
5   Huck. Then they parted and started for home.

When Tom climbed in at his bedroom window the night was nearly gone. He undressed very carefully, and fell asleep feeling pleased that nobody knew he had been out. He did not know that Sid was awake. He was
10   snoring gently, pretending to be asleep, but he had been awake for an hour or more.

When Tom woke, Sid was dressed and gone. There was a late sort of feeling in the air. He was surprised. Why hadn't they called him as they usually did?
15   Something was wrong. In five minutes he was dressed and downstairs, feeling sore and tired. The family had finished breakfast and were sitting round the table. No one would speak to Tom. After breakfast his aunt took him on one side. Tom felt sure he was going to be
20   beaten. But instead his aunt started to cry, and asked him how he could be so unkind to her.
This was much worse than a beating.
Tom asked her to forgive him
and promised to try to be
25   a better boy in future.
He felt too unhappy
to even feel angry
with Sid, who had
told Aunt Polly
30   about him.

He went sadly to school that morning. He felt even worse when he found that his new friend, Becky Thatcher, did not want to talk to him any more. Someone must have told her how bad he was.

Muff Potter is caught

By midday the whole village knew about the terrible killing of Doctor Robinson. The school master gave a holiday for the afternoon. Everyone would have thought it strange if he had not.

A knife had been found close to the body of the murdered doctor. It was said that it belonged to Muff Potter. Someone had seen Potter washing himself in the river at about one or two o'clock in the morning. He had run away at once. The town had been searched, but he could not be found.

Everybody was going towards the graveyard. Tom forgot his troubles and joined the crowd. When he arrived there, someone squeezed his arm. He turned, and his eyes met Huckleberry's. They both turned away at once, wondering if anyone had noticed them looking at each other. But everybody was talking, and looking at the awful scene in front of them.

'Poor young man.'

'This should be a lesson to grave-robbers.'

'Muff Potter will be hanged for this if they catch him.'

Now Tom began to shake with fright from head to toe, for he had noticed Injun Joe in the crowd. At this moment the crowd began to move, and voices shouted, 'It's him. It's him. He's coming himself.'

'Who? Who?' shouted people in the crowd.

'Muff Potter.'

'He's stopped. Look out, he's turning away. Don't let him get away.'

People in the branches of the trees over Tom's head said he wasn't trying to get away. He just looked puzzled.

'He wanted to have a quiet look at his work,' said one person close to Tom. 'He didn't expect to find anybody here.'

The crowd parted, and the Sheriff came through, leading Potter by the arm. The poor man looked very frightened.

'I didn't do it, friends,' he cried, 'on my word of honour, I didn't do it.'

'Who says you did?' shouted a voice.

Potter looked around him. He saw Injun Joe. Suddenly he knew what had happened. 'Oh, Injun Joe,' he cried, 'you promised me you'd never …'

'Is this your knife, Potter?' said the Sheriff, holding the knife in front of his face.

Potter would have fallen if they had not caught him. Then he said, 'I thought that if I didn't come back and get it, something would go wrong.' He shook all over. 'Tell them, Joe, tell them. It's no use keeping quiet any more.'

Then Huckleberry and Tom stood dumb and staring as they heard that liar, Injun Joe, tell his story. Every minute they expected God to strike him dead for his lies, but nothing happened. They almost decided to break their promise to each other, and save the prisoner's life. But when Injun Joe had finished, and he still stood alive and whole, they felt he must have sold himself to Satan, king of all the devils. If Satan was helping Injun Joe, it would be stupid to go against such power as that, they thought.

'Why didn't you leave? What did you want to come here for?' somebody asked Potter.

'I couldn't help it. I couldn't help it,' cried Potter. 'I wanted to run away, but I couldn't seem to come anywhere but here.'

Injun Joe repeated his story, just as calmly, a few minutes later, even though he had sworn on the Bible to tell the truth. The boys were now quite sure that he had sold himself to Satan, and because of this he was especially interesting to them. They made up their minds to watch him at night, if they got the chance. Perhaps they would see Injun Joe and his terrible Master together.

Injun Joe helped to lift the body of the murdered man and put it in a cart. It was whispered through the crowd that the young doctor's wound bled a little. The boys hoped that this might make people believe Injun Joe had done the killing. But more than one person said the bleeding started when Muff Potter was standing close to the body.

Tom is unwell

Tom's awful secret kept him awake for a long time after this. At breakfast one morning, Sid said, 'Tom, you move around and talk in your sleep so much that you keep me awake.'

Tom went white and looked at the floor.

'It's a bad sign,' said Aunt Polly. 'What is worrying you, Tom?'

'Nothing. Nothing I know of.' But his hand shook so that he spilled his coffee.

'And you do say such funny things,' went on Sid.
'Last night you said, "It's blood, it's blood, that's what
it is." You said that over and over. And you said, "Don't
hurt me, I'll tell." Tell what? What is it you'll tell?'

5 Tom began to feel faint. Goodness knows what might
have happened if Aunt Polly hadn't come to Tom's
rescue, without really knowing it.

'It's that awful murder. I dream about it nearly every
night myself. Sometimes I dream that I did it,' she said.

10 Mary said she had
bad dreams, too. Sid
seemed satisfied.

After that, Tom said he had toothache. He tied up his
jaws every night for a week. That would stop him

15 talking in his sleep, he thought. He never knew that
Sid watched him every night. He often slipped the
bandage free and leaned close to Tom to listen to what
he said. Then he put the bandage back again. If Sid
managed to make any sense out of Tom's words he

20 never told anyone.

Every day Tom went to the window of the village
prison-house to give the 'murderer' some food or some
other small gifts. It made Tom feel better, helping
Muff Potter in this way.

25 Tom now had other things on his mind.
Becky Thatcher had stopped coming to school. Even
though she refused to speak to him, Tom still liked her
a lot. He couldn't bear to think of her being sick.

What if she should die? He no longer enjoyed playing
with the other boys, and his aunt began to get worried
about him. She tried all sorts of medicines on him. She
gave him cold baths, then hot baths, but he still looked
pale and unhappy. She heard of a new medicine called 5
Pain-killer, so she decided to try this on poor Tom.

Tom soon had enough of all these medicines. He
thought that if he pretended to like Pain-killer, his aunt
might leave him alone for a while. He asked for it so
often that she finally told him to help himself. She 10
watched the bottle, and the medicine really did
disappear. What she did not know was that Tom was
pouring it into a crack in the sitting-room floor.

One morning Tom got to school very early. He
waited at the school gate instead of going to play with 15
his friends. He was sick, he said, and he looked it. He
seemed to be looking everywhere, but he was really
looking down the road.

Soon Jeff Thatcher, Becky's brother, came in sight,
but Becky was not with him. Tom turned sadly away, 20
and went into the empty school house to think. After
a short while he looked out of the window and saw
her in the yard. At once he ran outside and began
shouting and laughing with the other boys. He did
everything he could to make her notice him. But she 25
never looked his way. He went closer, took a boy's hat
and threw it up on to the school house roof. Then he
ran through a group of boys and fell over, nearly
knocking Becky down. She turned her back on him and
walked to the other side of the yard. As she went he 30
heard her say, 'Some people think they're very clever,
always showing off.'

Tom's face turned red. He picked himself up and
walked out of the yard, away from school. He felt very
unhappy.

5

JACKSON'S ISLAND

Pirates

By the time the bell rang for the beginning of school that morning, Tom was far away. He had decided that nobody loved him. Nobody would miss him. They would all be sorry when they found out what they had made him do.

He met another boy, his friend Joe Harper. Joe was also very unhappy. He had just been beaten by his mother. She thought he had drunk some cream. He said he had never tasted it and knew nothing about it, but she beat him anyway. It was easy to understand that she was tired of him and wished him to go. Joe was quite ready to run away with Tom.

The two boys decided to go to Jackson's Island, which was about three miles down the Mississippi river. They would live there and be pirates. They searched for Huckleberry Finn, and he agreed to go with them. They arranged to meet at midnight, two miles up river from St Petersburg, at a lonely spot on the river bank. There was a small log raft there which they would use to get across the river. Each boy was to bring hooks and lines for fishing, and as much food as he could.

At midnight Tom arrived at the meeting place. He brought a boiled ham with him. Joe had brought a side of bacon. It weighed a lot and he was very tired after carrying it. Huck had a saucepan and some tobacco.

Tom said it would be no good starting out without some fire. That was a wise thought, because they had no matches. They saw a fire on a large boat close to the bank, and went very quietly to take a piece of it. Luckily all the men from the boat were in the village.

At last they pushed the raft into the water and started
on their great adventure. They had a long way to go.
At St Petersburg the river Mississippi is a mile wide, and
the water runs fast and
strong. Jackson Island
is on the other side.

5

The raft floated down the
river. Tom stood in the middle and
gave the orders. The other boys had an oar
each, one at the front, the other at the back. Slowly   10
they pushed the raft through the water across the river.

An hour later they reached the island They took their
food from the raft and placed it on the shore. They
made a tent out of an old sail from the raft, to keep
the food sheltered They would sleep outside in the   15
open, as all good pirates do.

They built a fire against a big log, and cooked some
bacon for their supper. It was wonderful to be free, and
they said they would never go back home.

'Isn't this fun?' said Joe.   20

'It's wonderful,' replied Tom.

'What do pirates have to do?' asked Huck.

Tom said, 'Oh, they just have a good time. They go
on ships and take the money. Then they take it to their
island and bury it in awful places where there are ghosts   25
and things to watch it.'

They talked for a while about pirates and the things
they would do, then began to feel sleepy. But before

they slept, Tom and Joe began to feel a little fearful that
it had been wrong to run away. And what about the
meat they had stolen? They had taken things before, of
course, but this was somehow different. This was just
5   plain stealing. Each promised himself that he would
never steal again, and fell into a peaceful sleep.

Someone has drowned

Tom was the first to wake next morning. For a minute
he could not think where he was. He rubbed his eyes
10   and looked around him. Then he remembered. Joe and
Huck were still asleep, but it did not take long to wake
them. They ran to the river, and found that the raft had
floated away during the night. This did not worry them
at all and they were soon very hungry. While Joe cut
15   some bacon for breakfast, Tom and Huck went off to
catch some fish. They were lucky, and brought back
several large fish to cook with the bacon. This was the
best meal they had ever tasted.

After breakfast they set off to see the island. They
20   found it was about three miles long and a quarter of a
mile wide. They had a swim every hour, so it was the
middle of the afternoon before they got back to their
camp. They were too hungry to stop to fish, but had a
good meal of cooked ham.

25   As they sat talking, they heard a strange noise, far
away.

'What is it?' said Joe.

'I wonder,' said Tom in a whisper.

'Let's go and see.'

30   They jumped to their feet and hurried to the shore.
They hid behind some bushes near the water's edge
and looked out over the water. A small ferry-boat was
going backwards and forwards, crowded with people.

There were many small boats beside it, but it was too far away to see what the men in them were doing. Soon, some white smoke burst from the ferry-boat's side, and a noise was heard, like thunder, far away.

'I know now,' said Tom, 'somebody's been drowned.'

'That's right,' said Huck. 'They did that last summer when Billy Turner got drowned. They fire a big gun over the water and that makes the body come to the top.'

'I wish I was over there now,' said Joe.

'I do, too,' said Huck. 'I'd love to know who it is.'

The boys still listened and watched. Suddenly a thought flashed through Tom's mind.

'Boys, I know who's drowned. It's us.'

What a wonderful feeling that gave them. People were missing them, hearts were breaking for them and everyone must be feeling sorry for what they had done to these poor boys.

Tom hears some news

The ferry-boat went away at last, and the pirates went back to their camp. They were very excited about all the trouble they must be causing back at the village. They caught fish for supper, and sat talking about what the people back home must be saying about them. But when it grew dark, they stopped talking and sat looking into the fire. The excitement was gone now. Tom and Joe both thought of some people at home who might not be enjoying this joke.

At last Huck began to snore. Joe followed next. Tom lay still and watched them.

When the two boys were asleep, Tom did something very strange. He went home. It was a long way to go, and it was quite difficult because they had lost the raft.

Tom had to swim to the side of the river nearest the island. Then he walked to the ferry at St Petersburg. He used the ferry to cross the river, but no one saw him. It was dark and Tom knew where to hide.

Tom wanted to know what his Aunt Polly, and his brother and sister were doing. Late that night he got into the house without being seen. The family were in Aunt Polly's room, and Tom heard them talking about him. They thought he was dead, and they were all very sad indeed, even Sid. Aunt Polly said there would be a funeral for the poor dead boys next Sunday. When Tom heard that, his blood ran cold. He did not like to hear about his own funeral. But that gave him an idea.

Very quietly he crept out of the house. He went back to the island. When he arrived the boys were still sleeping. They did not know anything about his long journey.

Tom slept all through the morning of the next day. After dinner the three of them went to search for turtle eggs.

They went about pushing sticks into the sand by the river, and when they found a soft place they dug with their hands. Sometimes they would find fifty or sixty eggs in one hole. They were quite round and white, and about half the size of a chicken's egg. They had a huge fried egg supper that night, and more eggs for 5 breakfast on Friday morning. Then they went swimming again and played marbles on the sand. They sat quietly for a while, each deep in his own thoughts. Tom found himself writing 'Becky' in the sand with his big toe. He scratched it out and was angry with himself for his 10 weakness.

Huck and Joe want to leave

Joe was so homesick he could hardly hide it. He was very nearly in tears. Huck was sad too, and Tom felt unhappy but tried not to show it. He had a secret. He 15 wasn't ready to tell it to them yet, but if the boys didn't cheer up, he might have to tell them soon.

He said cheerfully, 'I expect there have been pirates on this island before, boys. We'll look round it again. They've hidden treasure here somewhere. How would 20 you like to find a chest full of gold and silver, hey?'

But the boys did not reply. Joe sat pushing a stick into the sand, and looking very unhappy. At last he said, 'Let's give up, boys. I want to go home. It's so lonely here.' 25

'Oh, no, Joe. You'll feel better soon,' said Tom. 'Just think of all the fishing we can do here.'

'I'm not interested in fishing. I want to go home.'

'But Joe, there's no other place like this for swimming.'

'Swimming's no good. I don't seem to care for that 30 when there's no one to say I mustn't do it. I'm going home.'

'You baby. You want to see your mother, I suppose.'

'Yes, I *do* want to see my mother, and you would too, if you had one. I'm not a baby any more than you are.'

'Well, we'll let the cry-baby go home to his mother, won't we, Huck? Poor thing, does it want to see its mother? And so it shall. *You* like it here, don't you, Huck? We'll stay, won't we?'

Huck said, 'Y-e-s,' but not as if he really meant it.

'I'll never speak to you again as long as I live, Tom Sawyer,' said Joe. 'There now.' And he moved away and began to dress himself.

'Who cares?' said Tom. 'Nobody wants you to. Go along home and get laughed at. Oh, you're a nice pirate. Huck and I aren't cry-babies. We'll stay, won't we, Huck? Let him go if he wants to. We can manage without him.'

He looked at Huck, but Huck could not bear it, and looked away.

'I want to go too, Tom. It was getting lonely anyway, but now it will be worse. Let's go too, Tom.'

'I won't. You can all go if you want to. I mean to stay.'

'Tom, I'd better go.'

'Well, go on then. Who's stopping you?'

Huck began to pick up his clothes.

'Tom, I wish you'd come too,' he said. 'You think it over. We'll wait for you when we get to the shore.'

'You'll have to wait a very long time,' replied Tom.

The great secret

Huck started sadly to walk away, and Tom stood looking after him. He hoped the boys would stop, but they still walked slowly on. Tom suddenly realized that it was very lonely. He ran after his friends, shouting, 'Wait, wait. I want to tell you something.'

They stopped and turned round. When he got to where they were he began to tell them his secret. When he had finished they shouted with joy, and asked him why he hadn't told them about it before. They wouldn't have started to go home if they had known about his secret plans.

They went happily back to their camp, and after eating an egg and fish dinner, played and talked until it was time to go to sleep.

That night it poured with rain and there was a terrible storm. The thunder roared and the lightning flashed for a long time. It was so bad that the boys had to hide in the tent until it was over.

Everything in the camp got wet, but luckily there was still a little of the fire left alight. It had burned so deeply into the log against which they had built it, that a small piece under the log had been sheltered from the rain. They piled on some dry bits of wood and soon had it burning again. They dried their boiled ham and had a good meal. As the sun came out, they lay on the sand to dry.

During the morning they began to feel homesick again, but Tom did his best to cheer them up. He told them to remember their great secret, and then he got them interested in a new idea. This was to stop being pirates for a while and be Indians for a change. It kept them busy all that day.

6

THE RETURN

A strange funeral

Saturday afternoon was sunny and peaceful, but there was no happiness in the village. The Harpers and Aunt Polly's family were feeling very sad. Everyone in
5 the village was quiet and unhappy. Even the children were not enjoying their holiday as usual. Becky Thatcher walked around the empty school yard wishing she had not been so nasty to Tom. Now she would never see him again to tell him how sorry she was.

10 The next morning, when the Sunday school hour was finished, the church bell began to ring slowly and sadly, as it does for a funeral. The people from the village began to gather at the church. They talked in whispers about the sad thing which had happened. All was quiet.
15 No one could remember when the church had been so full before. Aunt Polly entered with Sid and Mary. The Harper family followed, all dressed in black. Everyone in the church stood up until these two families reached their seats. There were sounds of people crying, and
20 the minister lifted up his hands and prayed. After this they all sang a hymn, and then the minister gave a talk about the poor, dead boys. It was all so sad. Everyone was in tears.

Suddenly there was a noise at the church door. The
25 minister raised his wet eyes above his handkerchief, and looked. His mouth opened wide with surprise. First one person, and then another turned to look towards the back of the church, too. Soon everyone was staring. They stared at the three dead boys who began
30 to march slowly up the aisle. Tom was in the lead,

then Joe and Huck followed
behind. They had been
hidden at the back of
the church, listening to
their own funeral.

Aunt Polly, Mary and the
Harpers threw themselves on
the boys, hugging and kissing
their loved ones. Poor Huck stood still, not knowing
what to do or where to hide. He started to move away, 10
but Tom took him by the arm and said, 'Aunt Polly, it's
not fair. Somebody's got to be glad to see Huck.'

'And so they shall. I'm glad to see him, poor
motherless thing.' And Aunt Polly began hugging Huck,
which made him feel very uncomfortable. 15

Suddenly the minister shouted at the top of his voice,
'Let us thank God by singing the hymn "Praise God
from whom all blessings flow." SING, everyone, and
put your hearts in it.' And they did.

When Tom returned to school, he found all the 20
children talking about his adventure, and secretly
wishing they could have done it themselves.

So the days passed by, until it was the end of school
and the holidays began. Tom had made friends with
Becky Thatcher once more, and they played happily 25
together until she went to stay in Constantinople with
her parents. Then Tom caught a fever and was very sick
for three weeks.

The trial

It was time for Muff Potter to be tried for the murder
of Doctor Robinson. The whole village was talking
about it, and Tom felt very frightened. He found Huck
5 and took him to a quiet place where they could talk.

'Huck, have you told anybody about that?'

'About what?'

'You know what.'

'Oh, of course I haven't.'

10 'Never a word?'

'Never a word, I promise. What makes you ask?'

'I was afraid, that's all.'

'Tom, if Injun Joe found out, we wouldn't be alive
for long, you know that.'

15 'I know. Let's swear again to keep quiet about it,
Huck. Just to make sure.'

So they promised again to say nothing to anyone of
what they knew about the murder.

'Poor Muff Potter,' said Huck. 'I don't think he's got
20 a chance of being set free. Don't you feel sorry for him
sometimes?'

'Yes, I do. He's always been kind to me. He's mended
my kites, and given me fish and tied hooks on my
fishing lines. I wish we could do something to help him.'

25 The boys had a long talk, and then went to the little
prison. There were no guards, and Potter's room was
on the ground floor. They went to the window and gave
him some tobacco and matches.

As always, he was very grateful for their presents.

30 'You boys have been very kind to me, and I thank
you for it,' he said. 'You didn't forget me, like everybody
else in the village. I did a very bad thing, and now I've
got to be punished. That's only right. But don't you
boys ever get drunk, then you'll never end up in here.'

Tom went home very unhappy, and that night he had terrible dreams. The next day and the day after he stood outside the court-room, wanting to go in, but not feeling brave enough. He listened to the talk of people coming away from the court, and felt even worse. It seemed that Injun Joe had not changed his story. No one could prove that what he said was not true. At the end of the second day, it seemed clear that the jury would be sure Muff Potter was the murderer. Muff Potter would be found guilty.

That night Tom stayed out very late. When he got home he climbed into his bedroom through the window. He was very excited and it was hours before he fell asleep.

Tom tells the truth

The next morning, all the village crowded in to the court-house. This was the great day. After a long wait the jury walked in and took their places. A short time after that, Potter was brought in. He looked pale and without hope. He was made to sit where everybody could stare at him. Injun Joe was in court, too. The judge arrived, and the court was ready to begin.

One man told the court that he had seen Potter washing in the river on the night of the murder. Another man proved that the knife had been found next to the dead body. A third man said that he had seen Potter with that knife and he knew it was Potter's knife. Potter's lawyer did not ask any questions, and things looked very bad for the poor man. Then a voice said, 'Call Thomas Sawyer.'

Every head in the court-room turned to look at Tom as he made his way to the witness stand. He swore on the Bible to tell the truth.

Potter's lawyer stood up and began to ask Tom some questions.

'Thomas Sawyer, where were you on the seventeenth of June, about the hour of midnight?'

Tom looked quickly at Injun Joe's face, and he could not speak. Everyone was listening breathlessly, but the words refused to come. After a few minutes, however, he managed to whisper, 'In the graveyard.'

'A little louder, please. Don't be afraid.'

'In the graveyard.'

'Were you anywhere near Horse William's grave?'

'Yes, sir.'

'How near were you?'

'As near as I am to you.'

'Were you hidden or not?'

'I was hidden.'

'Where?'

'Behind the trees near the grave.'

'Was anyone with you?'

'Yes, sir, I went there with …'

'Wait, wait a minute. Never mind telling us your friend's name. We will hear from him at the proper time. Did you carry anything with you?' Tom did not want to answer. 'Speak up, my boy. What did you take there?'

'Only a — a dead cat.'

There was a little laughter at this, which stopped as the judge raised his hand.

'Now, my boy, tell us everything that happened. Don't leave anything out, and don't be afraid.'

Tom began, slowly at first, but as he went on he found he could speak more easily. In a little while there was not a sound in the court-room, except the sound of his own voice. Every eye was fixed on him as his audience listened to the terrible story. Tom got to the part where the murder happened.

'I saw the doctor hit Muff Potter with the piece of wood. Muff Potter fell to the ground. Then Injun Joe picked up Muff Potter's knife and …'

Crash! Quick as lightning Injun Joe jumped through the window and was gone. 5

So Tom was a hero once more. He had saved Muff Potter's life. Tom felt happy during the day. Everyone was very kind to him, and said nice things about him. But his nights were terrible. His dreams were full of Injun Joe. It was no longer fun to go out at night. 10

Poor Huck felt frightened, too. Tom had told the lawyer the whole story the night before the last day of the trial. Huck was afraid that if Injun Joe got to know about it, he would be in great danger.

A TREASURE HUNT

The haunted house

Nobody had seen Injun Joe since the day he jumped
through the courtroom window. A reward was offered
to anyone who could find him. The countryside had
5 been searched, but Injun Joe had not been found. The
days passed slowly.

Tom and Huck decided to try and find some buried
treasure. Tom was sure that there was a lot of it around.
They spent whole days digging holes in many parts of
10 the countryside, but without any luck. Then Tom said
that they should dig in the haunted house.

'The haunted house. Oh, Tom I don't think I like
that,' said Huck. 'Haunted houses are full of ghosts, and
I don't like ghosts. They creep up on you suddenly and
15 make awful noises.'

'Yes, but ghosts don't come out until night time,
Huck. They wouldn't trouble us during the day.'

Huck had to agree with this,
so they arranged to meet at
20 midday the next day.

When they reached the
haunted house on the next
afternoon they both felt a
little frightened. It looked
25 very ghostly. The walls
were falling down,
there was no glass in
the windows, and
grass grew
30 everywhere.

They crept to the door and looked in. Inside they saw
a very old fire-place, a broken staircase and plenty of dust
and spider's webs. They entered quietly, talking in
whispers. They were ready to run at the smallest sound.
But once inside, the house did not seem so frightening.   5
They looked around, feeling quite brave, and then decided
to take a look upstairs. They threw their tools into a corner,
and went up. There was nothing exciting to see up there,
and they were just about to go down when …

'Sh,' said Tom.   10

'What is it?' whispered Huck, turning white with
fright.

'Sh! There! Do you hear it?'

'Yes. Come on, let's run.'

'Keep still. Don't move an inch. They're coming   15
towards the door.'

The boys stretched themselves on the floor with their
eyes to holes in the wooden boards. They could see
downstairs from there, but no-one could see them. They
lay there waiting, feeling very frightened.   20

'They've stopped. No, they're coming in. Here they
are. Don't whisper another word, Huck. My goodness,
I wish I was out of this place.'

Two men entered. 'There's the old deaf and dumb
Spaniard who's been about the village once or twice   25
recently,' Tom thought to himself. 'But I've never seen
the other man before.'

The other man wore rags, and looked unfriendly. The
Spaniard was wearing a simple coat made from a
blanket. He had a white beard and moustache, and   30
white hair. As they came in, the other man was talking
in a low voice. They sat down on the ground, facing
the door, with their backs to the wall.

'No,' he said, 'I've thought about it, and I don't like
it. It's dangerous.'   35

'Dangerous?' said the 'deaf and dumb' Spaniard, to
the great surprise of the boys. 'Coward!'

This voice made the boys shake all over. It was
Injun Joe's voice. There was silence for some time. Then
Joe said, 'Listen, you go back up the river where you
belong. Wait there till you hear from me. I'll go into the
village one more time, for a look around. We'll do that
"dangerous" job later, when I think the time is right.
Then we'll both go to Texas.'

The other man agreed. Joe said he was tired and
wanted to sleep, and told the other man to keep watch.
He was soon snoring. His friend watched him for a
time, but soon he was asleep too.

The boys breathed more easily.

'Now's our chance, come on,' whispered Tom.

'I can't. If they woke up, I'd die of fright.'

Treasure!

At last Tom got up very slowly and softly, and started
to move across the floor. He thought he could get across
the room without making any noise. But the first step
he took made one of the floor-boards creak so loudly
that he sat down again, almost dead with fright. He did
not try to do that again. The boys lay there counting the
seconds, until it seemed to them they would lie there
for ever. Then they noticed that the sun was setting.

Now one of the snorers stopped. Injun Joe sat up
and stared around and saw his friend was fast asleep.
He kicked him and said, 'You're a fine guard, aren't
you? Lucky nothing's happened. It's nearly time for us
to be moving. What shall we do with the money we've
got left?'

'I don't know. Leave it here as we've always done, I
think. It's no use taking it away until we go south. Six
hundred and fifty dollars in silver is too much to carry.'

'Well, all right, it won't be any trouble to come here again.'

'No, but I think we should come at night, like we used to, it's better.'

'Yes. But it may be some time before I get a chance to do that job. Accidents might happen. We'll bury it properly, and bury it deep.'

'Good idea,' said his friend, getting up and crossing the room. He went to the old fire-place and lifted up a stone at the back of the fire. He pulled out a bag from which he took out twenty or thirty dollars for himself and as much for Injun Joe. Injun Joe was in the corner, digging with his knife.

The boys forgot all their fears at once. With bright eyes they watched every movement. What luck! Six hundred dollars was enough money to make quite a few boys rich.

This was a wonderful way to carry out a treasure hunt. They knew exactly where to dig.

Joe's knife struck something.

'Hello,' he said.

'What is it?' asked his friend.

'A rotten piece of wood. No, I believe it's a box. Here, help me to get it up. Never mind, I've made a hole in it.'

He reached in his hand and drew it out.

'Man, it's money.'

The two men examined the handful of coins. They were gold. The boys above were as excited themselves.

Joe's friend said, 'Let's get the box up quickly. There's an old pick over in the corner, I saw it a minute ago.'

Injun Joe comes up the stairs

He ran and brought the boys' pick and shovel. Injun Joe took the pick, looked at it for a minute or two, shook his head, and began to use it.

5   The box was soon lying on the floor. It was not very large. It had iron bands round it, and had been very strong before the years had rotted it away.

'There are thousands of dollars here,' said Injun Joe.

'People used to say that the Murrel gang used this

10   place one summer,' said his friend.

'I know,' replied Injun Joe, 'and this looks like their money.'

'Now you don't need to do that job.'

The Indian looked at his friend, fiercely.

15   'I'm not doing the job just for money,' he said. 'It's revenge I want, and I'll need your help. When it's finished we'll go to Texas. Go home to your wife and children and wait till you hear from me.'

'Well, if you say so. What shall we do with this? Shall

20   we bury it again?'

'Yes.' (The boys were very pleased to hear this.) 'No, wait. I'd nearly forgotten. What are that pick and shovel doing here?' (The boys were sick with fright.) 'Who brought them here, and where have they gone? Have

25   you heard anybody? Seen anybody? We'd be fools to bury it again and let them find the ground newly dug. We'll take it to my hiding place.'

'Why, of course. We should have thought of that before. You mean number one?'

30   'No, number two, under the cross.'

Injun Joe got up and went about from window to window, carefully looking out. At last he said, 'Who could have brought those tools here? Do you think they can be upstairs?'

The boys nearly died from fright. Injun Joe put his hand on his knife, turned and made his way to the staircase. There was the sound of footsteps coming up the stairs. The boys were just about to jump up and run for their lives, when there was a crash. The stairs broke and Injun Joe landed on the ground on a pile of rotten wood. He stood up. He was very angry. His friend said, 'If there is anybody up there, let them stay. Who cares? It will be dark in fifteen minutes. I think the person who brought those things in here saw us coming and thought we were ghosts or devils or something. They'll have run away by now. I expect they are miles away.'

Joe agreed with his friend. In a short while, when it was dark, they left the house. They went towards the river, taking their silver and the box of gold coins with them.

Tom and Huck got up and watched them through holes in the wall. They jumped to the ground safely and went towards the village. They didn't talk much. They were very angry with themselves for leaving the pick and shovel in sight. If Joe hadn't seen those, he would never have worried about anyone else being there. He would have buried the silver and gold, and gone away. Then the boys could have dug it up. Oh, what bad luck! They agreed to look out for that Spaniard when he came to the village. Then they could follow him to 'number two', though they did not know where that might be. Then Tom had an awful thought.

'Revenge? What if he means *us*, Huck?'

'Oh, don't,' said Huck, nearly falling down in fear.

They talked about it. As they entered the village they agreed to believe that he might have meant somebody else. Or perhaps he had only meant Tom, because it had been Tom who had spoken at the trial.

THE ROOM AT THE INN

Where is number two?

Poor Tom had very bad dreams that night. In his dreams, four times he had his hands on the treasure, and four times he lost it. When he woke next morning,
5 everything that had happened the day before seemed like a dream, too. He got up, had his breakfast and went to find Huck.

Huck was sitting on a raft with his feet in the water. He looked most unhappy. Tom decided not to be the
10 first to talk about what had happened yesterday. If Huck said nothing about it, it must have been a dream.

'Hello, Huck.'

'Hello yourself.'

There was silence for a minute.

15 'Tom, if we hadn't taken those tools with us we'd have got the money. Oh, isn't it awful?' said Huck.

'It wasn't a dream, then,' said Tom. 'Somehow I almost wish it was.'

'What wasn't a dream?'

20 'Oh, those things that happened yesterday.'

'We were lucky those stairs broke down. I've had dreams about that all night, with that devil, the Spaniard, in all of them.'

'We must try to find him, and the money.'

25 'Tom, we'll never find him. I'm not sure I want to see him again, anyway.'

'I know, I'm a bit frightened, too. But I'd like to see him and follow him to his number two.'

'Number two. Yes, I've been thinking about that. I
30 don't know what he meant by that. What do you think it is?'

'I don't know,' replied Tom. He thought for a minute, then said, 'Perhaps it's the number of a house.'

'No, Tom, it can't be that. If it is, it's not in this place. There aren't any numbers here in St Petersburg.'

'You're right. Let me think again. Could it be the number of a room, in an inn, you know?'

'Oh, that's a good idea. There are only two inns here. We can find out very quickly.'

'You stay here, Huck, till I come.'

Tom went off at once. He was gone for half an hour. He found that in the best inn, room number two belonged to a young lawyer. He had lived there for a long time, and was still staying in the room. In the other inn, room number two was a mystery. The inn-keeper's son said it was kept locked all the time. He had never seen anyone come out of it except at night. He had noticed that there was a light in there the night before.

'That's what I've found out, Huck. I think this is the number two we're looking for.'

'I think you're right, Tom. Now what are you going to do?'

Tom thought for a long time. Then he said, 'I'll tell you. The back door of that number two room is the door that opens into the little street between the inn and the old brick shop. Now you get hold of all the keys you can find. I'll take all of Auntie's. The first dark night, we shall go there and try to unlock that door. And don't forget to keep a look-out for Injun Joe. He said he was coming back here, remember? If you see him, follow him. If he doesn't go to room number two, then it's not the right place.'

Thursday night

That night Tom and Huck were ready for their adventure. They waited near the inn until after nine

o'clock. One of them watched the street. The other
watched the inn door, from a safe distance, of course.
Nobody left the street or entered it. Nobody looking
like the Spaniard entered or left the inn door.

5　　　　The moon was very bright, so Tom went home. He
asked Huck to come and make a noise like a cat under
his window if it grew dark enough. Then he would slip
out and they could try the keys. But the night stayed
clear, and Huck gave up his watch and went to bed in
10　an empty sugar barrel at about midnight.

　　　On Tuesday, the boys had the same bad luck. Also
on Wednesday. But on Thursday night the sky was
covered with clouds. Tom crept out with his aunt's old
tin lamp, and a large towel to cover it with. He hid the
15　lamp in Huck's sugar barrel and began to watch. An
hour before midnight the inn lights went out. Nobody
had entered or left the alley.

　　　Tom got his lamp, lit it in the barrel
and covered it with the towel.
20　The boys crept towards the
inn. Huck stood on
guard and Tom felt
his way carefully
into the alley.

Huck waited and waited. It seemed hours since Tom had disappeared. Something must have happened to him. Perhaps he was dead. Suddenly there was a flash of light, and Tom came rushing by him.

'Run,' he said, 'run for your life.'

Is the money there?

He need not have repeated it. Once was enough for Huck. The boys never stopped until they reached an old building at the lower end of the village. As soon as Tom got his breath he said, 'Huck, it was awful. I tried two of the keys as softly as I could, but they made an awful noise. I could hardly get my breath, I was so frightened. They wouldn't turn in the lock. Without noticing what I was doing, I put my hand on the door handle and the door opened. It wasn't locked. I went in and shook off the towel, and oh, Huck.'

'What ... what did you see, Tom?'

'Huck, I almost stepped on to Injun Joe's hand.'

'No.'

'Yes. He was lying there, fast asleep on the floor.'

'What did you do? Did he wake up?'

'No, he never moved. I think he was drunk. I just picked up the towel and ran.'

'Tom, did you see that box?'

'Huck, I didn't wait to look around. I didn't see the box, I didn't see the cross. I didn't see anything but a bottle and a tin cup on the floor by Injun Joe.'

'Now that Injun Joe's drunk, it would be a good time to go and get that box.'

'Go on, then. You try,' said Tom.

Huck shook with fear.

'Well, no. I don't think so,' he said.

'And I don't think so, Huck. Only one bottle beside Injun Joe is not enough. If there had been three bottles, then he'd have been drunk enough and I'd do it.'

There was a long thoughtful silence. Then Tom said, 'Huck, let's not try any more until we're sure Injun Joe's not in there. If we watch every night, we'll be sure to see him go out some time. Then we'll go in and get that box.'

'I agree,' said Huck. 'I'll watch the whole night long, and I'll do it every night too, if you'll do the other part of the job.'

'All right, I will. All you've got to do is come up Hooper Street and call. If I'm asleep, throw a stone at the window. That will wake me. I must go home now. It will be morning in an hour or two. You go back and watch until it is light, will you?'

'I said I would, Tom, and I will. I'll watch every night for a year. I'll sleep all day and I'll watch the inn all night.'

'Good. Now where are you going to sleep?'

'At Ben Rogers' farm. He often lets me sleep there.'

'If I don't want you in the daytime, Huck, I'll let you sleep. Any time you see anything happening in the night, just come right round and call.'

9

THE PICNIC

McDougal's cave

Tom heard some very good news on Friday morning. His friend Becky Thatcher and her family had come back to St Petersburg the night before. He was so busy playing with Becky and his friends, that he almost forgot about Injun Joe and the treasure.

Becky's mother had arranged a picnic for Becky and her friends for the next day. Tom was so excited that he could not sleep. He hoped that Huck might come and call for him. Then they would find the treasure and he could show it to Becky the next day. But he was disappointed. No signal came that night.

At ten o'clock next morning a large group of children met outside Judge Thatcher's house. There were no parents. The children were thought to be safe with a few young ladies of eighteen, and a few young gentlemen of twenty-three. An old steam ferry-boat was to be used for the trip. Soon the happy crowd walked up the main street carrying heavy picnic baskets full of good things to eat. Sid was sick, so he had to stay at home, and Mary stayed behind to play with him. The last thing Mrs Thatcher said to Becky was, 'You won't get back till late. Perhaps you'd better stay all night with one of the girls that lives near the ferry landing, child.'

'Then I'll stay with Susy Harper, mother.'

'Very well, and mind you behave yourself, and don't be any trouble.'

As they walked along, Tom said to Becky, 'I'll tell you what we'll do. Instead of going to the Harpers, we'll climb up Cardiff Hill and stop at Widow Douglas's.

She'll have ice cream. She has it most days. And she'll be very glad if we go to see her.'

'Oh, that will be fun.'

Then Becky thought for a minute.

'But what will mother say?'

'How will she ever know?'

The girl thought again, then said slowly, 'I know it's wrong, but ...'

'Don't worry,' said Tom. 'Your mother won't know, and so what's the harm? All she wants is for you to be safe. I expect she would have said to go there, if she'd thought of it herself. I know she would.'

So they decided to say nothing to anybody about their plans for that evening.

The ferry-boat took them down the river for about three miles. It stopped near a wood, and they all ran off to explore. They played for a long time in the sun, and then they were glad to sit and eat all the things in the picnic baskets. After lunch they rested in the shade of the trees. Soon someone said, 'Who's ready to go to the cave?'

Everybody was. Candles were given out, and the children rushed up the hill. The mouth of the cave was high up the hillside. The opening looked like the letter A. There was a large wooden door at the entrance. The door was open. The candles were lit, and a long line of children started walking carefully down the main passage.

McDougal's cave was just a lot of crooked passages that ran into each other and out again and led nowhere. They went a very long way under the hill. You could walk for many days and nights, down into the earth, and never find the end of the cave. No-one knew where all the cave passages went. There were so many that it was impossible to know. Most of the young men knew some of the passages quite well, and no one usually went far beyond the known part. Tom Sawyer knew as much of the cave as anyone.

They walked down the passage for about three quarters of a mile. Then small groups began to run along a side path and jump out on their friends where the passages met again. It was great fun. They played games in the cave like this for a long time.

At last, one group after another came back to the mouth of the cave. They were tired and dirty, covered in candle wax, but very happy. It had been a very good day. They were surprised to find it was dark outside, for they had not thought of the time when they were inside the cave. The ferry bell had been ringing for half an hour. When the ferry-boat left, the only person who cared about the wasted time was the captain.

On Cardiff Hill

Huck was already watching the inn when the ferry-boat's lights went past on the river. There was no noise coming from it now, because all the children were nearly asleep.

The night was growing cloudy and dark. Ten o'clock came, and lights began to go out as people went to bed. Huck was alone with the silence and the ghosts. Eleven o'clock came, and the inn lights were put out. There was darkness everywhere now. Huck waited for what seemed a very long time, but nothing happened.

He began to wonder if it was any use waiting. Why not give it up and go to bed?

Then he heard a noise. In the alley a door closed softly. He went to the corner of the alley. The next minute two men brushed by him, and one seemed to have something under his arm. It must be that box. So they were going to take the treasure away. Why go and call Tom now? It would be silly. The men would get away with the box and never be found again. No, he would follow them by himself. He hoped it was dark enough for them not to see him. Huck stepped out and crept along behind the men. He let them keep far enough in front, so that he could just see them.

They turned along the river road, then turned left up another street. They went straight on until they came to the path that led up Cardiff Hill. Up the path they went. They passed by the old Welshman's house, half-way up the hill, without stopping. 'Good,' thought Huck, 'they are going to bury it in the old quarry.' But they didn't stop at the quarry. They went on, up to the top. They took a narrow path between tall bushes and were at once hidden in the darkness. Huck got closer to them now, for they would never be able to see him. After a while he stopped and listened. There was no sound of footsteps. Had he lost them? He was about to start running, when a man coughed, less than four feet away from him. Huck was very, very frightened. He stood there shaking. He knew where he was now. He was about five steps from the gate which led to Widow Douglas's place. 'If they bury it here,' he thought, 'it won't be hard to find.'

Now he heard a low voice, a very low voice. It was Injun Joe's.

'She's got friends there. There are lights on, late as it is.'

'I can't see any.'

This was that stranger's voice, the one in the haunted house.

Injun Joe's revenge

An awful feeling crept over Huck. This must be the 'revenge' job Injun Joe had spoken about. His first thought was to run away as fast as he could. Then he remembered that the Widow Douglas had been kind to him more than once. Perhaps these men were going to murder her. He wished he could go and tell her, but he knew he didn't dare. He thought all this, and more, in the short time between the stranger's last words and Injun Joe's next:

'That's because the bush is in the way. Look through here. Now you see, don't you?'

'Yes. Well, if there are people there, we'd better give up the idea.'

'Not I. I may never get another chance. I've told you, it's not the money I'm after, you can have it. But her husband was hard on me. He had me put in prison, but that's not all. He had me whipped in front of the whole town. Whipped! Do you understand? He's dead now. He died before I could have my revenge. By dying so soon he got the better of me. But I'll get my revenge on her, instead.'

'Oh, don't kill her. Don't do that.'

'Kill? Who said anything about killing? I would kill him if he was here, but not her. When you want to get revenge on a woman, you don't kill her. No, you go for her looks. You cut her face, her nose and ears.'

'By God, that's …'

'Keep your thoughts to yourself. It will be safest for you; I'll tie her to the bed. If she bleeds to death,

is that my fault? I'll not cry if she does. My friend, you will help me in this thing, that's why you are here. If you don't help me I'll kill you. Do you understand that? And if I have to kill you, I'll kill her. And then I don't
5 think anyone will be able to tell who did it.'

'Well, if it's got to be done, let's do it now.'

'Do it now? With people there? No, we'll wait till the lights are out. There's no hurry.'

The old Welshman

10 In the silence which followed, Huck began to move. He stepped back very carefully, making sure he did not slip. He took another step backwards, then another and another. A twig broke under his foot. His breath stopped and he listened. There was no sound. Now he
15 turned round. He turned himself as carefully as if he were a ship at sea, and then stepped quickly but carefully along. When he came to the quarry he felt safe, so he ran. Down, down he ran till he reached the Welshman's house. He banged on the door, and
20 soon the heads of the old man and his two large sons looked out of the windows.

'What's that noise? Who's banging? What do you want?'

'Let me in, quick.'

'Why, who are you?'

'Huckleberry Finn. Quick, let me in.'

'Huckleberry Finn, indeed,' said Mr Jones, the old Welshman. 'Not many people will open their doors when they hear that name. But let him in, boys, and let's find out what he has to say.'

'Please, don't ever tell anyone that I told you,' were Huck's first words when he got in. 'Please don't. I'd be killed. But she's been a good friend to me sometimes, and I want to tell. I will tell if you'll promise you won't ever say it was me.'

'Goodness,' said the old man, 'he has got something to tell, or he wouldn't act like this. Nobody here will ever tell, boy. Now what is the matter?'

Three minutes later the old man and his sons, carrying guns, were up the hill, and moving along the path quietly. Huck would not go along the path. He hid behind a big rock and listened. There was a long silence, and then suddenly he heard the noise of a gun firing. Huck waited no longer. He jumped up and ran down the hill as fast as his legs would carry him.

10

SUNDAY MORNING

Huck makes some friends

Next morning, before it was light, Huck made his way
up to the Welshman's house. He knocked on the door,
and a voice called, 'Who's there?'

5   Huck's frightened voice answered, 'Do please let me
in. It's only Huck Finn.'

'That's a name that can open the door of this house
night or day, boy. We are glad to see you,' said old
Mr Jones.

10   Huck was surprised. No one had ever spoken so
kindly to him before. The door was quickly opened and
he entered. The old man and his boys got dressed.

'Now, my boy, I hope you are hungry, because
breakfast will be ready soon. I and my two boys hoped
15   you'd come back here last night to stay with us.'

'I was very frightened,' said Huck, 'and I ran when
the guns went off. I didn't stop for three miles. I've
come now because I want to know what happened.
And I came before it got light because I didn't want to
20   meet those men, even if they were dead.'

'You do look as if you've had a bad night,' said the
old man. 'You can sleep here when you've had your
breakfast. No, they're not dead, we're sorry about that.
They got away from us. But we went down to the
25   village and told the police. They went off to guard the
river bank. The Sheriff and his men are going to search
in the woods. My boys will be joining them soon. I
wish we knew what they looked like. It would help a
lot. But you couldn't see what they were like in the
30   dark, could you, boy?'

'Oh, yes, I saw them in the village and followed them.'

'Good boy, tell me what they looked like.'

'One of them is the old deaf and dumb Spaniard that's been around here once or twice, and the other's a mean looking, ragged ...'

'That's enough, boy. We know the men. We saw them in the woods at the back of the widow's place one day, and they ran off when they saw us. Off with you, boys, and tell the Sheriff. You can have your breakfast later.'

The Welshman's sons got up to go. As they were leaving, Huck jumped up and said, 'Oh, please don't tell anybody it was me that told you. Oh, please.'

'All right, if you say so, Huck. But someone ought to know how brave you were.'

'Oh no, no. Please don't tell.'

When the young men had gone, the old Welshman said, 'They won't tell, and I won't. But why don't you want it known?'

Huck would not explain, but said that he already knew too much about one of those men. He didn't want the man to know, or he might kill him.

'How did you come to follow these men, boy? Were they doing something they shouldn't have been doing?'

Huck was silent while he thought of a good reply to the old man's question. Then he said, 'I couldn't sleep last night, so I went for a walk. I don't live anywhere special, you see. I came along the street at midnight, and these two men came past me. They had something under their arm, so I thought, they must have stolen it. One was smoking, and the other wanted a light. They stopped near me, and the match lit up their faces. I could see one was that deaf and dumb Spaniard, because he had a white beard, and the other one was a ragged-looking man.'

'Could you see the rags by the light of the match?'

This worried Huck for a minute. Then he said, 'Well, I don't know. It seemed as if I could.'

'Then they went on and you followed them.'

5   'Yes, I did. I wanted to see what they would do. They looked as if they were up to something bad. I followed them to Widow Douglas's place and hid near them in the dark. I heard the Spaniard say he'd spoil her looks, just like I told you and your two sons.'

10 'What? The deaf and dumb man said all that?'

Huck had made a terrible mistake. He was trying his best to keep the old man from guessing who the Spaniard might be. But it was no good.

'My boy,' said old Mr Jones at last, 'don't be afraid

15 of me. I won't hurt you. No, I'll protect you. This Spaniard is not deaf and dumb. You told me that without meaning to. You know something about that Spaniard that you want to keep hidden. Now trust me, tell me what it is. I won't let him harm you.'

20 Huck looked into the old man's honest eyes, and then bent over and whispered in his ear, 'He's not a Spaniard. He's Injun Joe.'

25 The old man jumped out of his chair.

'I should have known,' he said. 'When you talked about cutting noses and ears I thought you were making it up. I don't know of many people who would take revenge that way. But Injun Joe would.'

After breakfast there was a knock on the door. Huck got up and found a place to hide. He didn't want anyone to know he was there.

The Welshman opened the door, and several ladies and gentlemen came into the room. Among them was the Widow Douglas. The news had spread. The Welshman had to tell the story of the night to the visitors. The lady was very grateful for the old man's help.

'Don't say another word about it, madam,' he replied. 'There's another person that you should thank. He did far more for you than me and my boys. But he won't let me tell you his name. We wouldn't have been there if he hadn't told us about it.'

More visitors came, and the story had to be told again and again.

In church

There was no Sunday school during the day-school holiday, but everybody was early at church. News came that the two men had still not been found. When the meeting was over, Judge Thatcher's wife went to speak to Mrs Harper.

'Is my Becky going to sleep all day? I knew she would be very tired.'

'Your Becky?' said Mrs Harper.

'Yes. Didn't she stay with you last night?'

'Why, no.'

Mrs Thatcher turned pale and had to sit down, just as Aunt Polly passed by.

'Good morning, Mrs Thatcher. Good morning, Mrs Harper,' said Aunt Polly. 'I think my Tom must have stayed with one of you last night, and now he's afraid to come to church. Just wait till I see him.'

5   Mrs Thatcher shook her head and turned paler than ever.

'He didn't stay with us,' said Mrs Harper, beginning to look worried. Aunt Polly began to look frightened.

'Joe Harper, have you seen my Tom this morning?'

10   'No.'

'When did you last see him?'

Joe tried to remember, but was not sure. The people stopped moving out of church. Whispers went round, and everyone started looking worried. Children were

15   questioned, and the young ladies and gentlemen. They all said they had not noticed whether Tom and Becky were with the others on the way home. It was dark. No one thought of asking if anyone was missing. One young man at last said he was afraid they were still in

20   the cave. Mrs Thatcher and Aunt Polly began to cry.

The news spread from lip to lip, from group to group, from street to street, and in five minutes the bells were ringing and the whole village was out for the search. Injun Joe and his friend were forgotten. Horses were

25   got ready, boats hurriedly put into the water, the ferry-boat was ordered out. In less than an hour, two hundred men were going down the river and the roads towards the cave.

All that afternoon the village seemed empty and

30   dead. Many women visited Aunt Polly and Mrs Thatcher and tried to comfort them. All night the village waited for news. But when it was light the only word that came was, 'Send more candles and food.'

The old Welshman came home in the early morning.

35   He was covered in candle wax and mud, and was

very tired. He found Huck still in bed, sick with a fever.
All the doctors had gone to the cave, so the
Widow Douglas came to look after him. She still did
not know the part he had played in saving her from
the revenge of Injun Joe. 5

Early in the afternoon some of the men began to
come back to the village. Others were still carrying on
the search. It was said that every corner of the cave
was being looked into. Men were searching places that
had never been visited before. 10

For three terrible days and nights there was no more
news.

11

UNDER THE GROUND

Lost!

At the picnic Tom and Becky had gone along the dark paths of McDougal's cave with the rest of the children. Soon all the children began to play games, running around in the passages, hiding, and trying to catch one another. Tom and Becky joined in, of course. Then, after a while, they tired of the games and walked down a winding passage, holding their candles high.

Visitors to the cave had written their names, and the dates on the walls in candle smoke. Becky and Tom read some of them as they walked along. They were talking so much that it was a little while before they noticed that they were now in a part of the cave that had no writing on the wall. They used candle smoke to write their own names on the rock and walked on.

Soon they came to a place where a little stream of water was running. Over the years it had shaped the cave wall so it looked like a frozen waterfall. Tom went behind it to light it up with the candle so that Becky could see it better. Behind the stone waterfall he found an opening in the rock, leading downwards. At once he wanted to explore it. Becky agreed and together they started to walk down into the earth. They wound this way and that, far down into the cave, making smoke marks here and there to show them the way back. This was exciting. They would have a lot to tell the children above when they returned.

In one place they found a huge open space full of shining stalactites, as long and thick as a man's leg.

They walked around it and left by one of the many passages that opened into it. The next place they found was full of bats. There were thousands of them. The candle lights woke them up, and they flew at the candle flames. Tom knew this was dangerous, and took Becky's hand to hurry her away. He pulled her into the first opening he found, and not too soon. One of the bats had struck her candle out with its wings. The bats chased the children for quite a long way, but they ran into every new passage that they came to, and at last got away from them.

Then Tom found an underground lake. He wanted to explore around its edge, but he decided to sit down and rest first.

Now, for the first time the dark and the deep stillness of the place made the children afraid. Becky said, 'I didn't notice before, Tom, but it seems a long time since I heard any of the others.'

5 'You're right, Becky. We are down below them, and I don't know how far we have come. We can't hear them from here.'

Becky was worried.

'I wonder how long we've been down here, Tom?
10 We'd better start back.'

'Yes, I think we'd better.'

'Can you find the way, Tom? It's all mixed up and crooked to me.'

'I think I can find it, but remember the bats? If they
15 put out both our candles we'll be in trouble. Let's try some other way, so that we don't have to go through the place where the bats are.'

'Well, I hope we won't get lost. It would be so awful,' and Becky shook with fear at the thought of it.

20 They started off down a passage and went in silence for a long way. They kept looking at each new opening, hoping that they might remember being there before, but everything looked new to them. At last Becky said, 'Oh, Tom, never mind the bats. Let's go back that way.'

25 Tom stopped. 'Listen,' he said.

All was silent. There was no sound at all. Tom shouted. The noise was terrible. As it faded away, it sounded like a frightening laugh.

'Oh, don't do it again, Tom, it's too awful,' said Becky.
30 'It is awful, but I'd better try, they might hear us, you know.' He shouted again. The children stood and listened, but there was no answer. Tom turned and hurried on. It was only a little while before Becky saw something was wrong. Tom could not find his way
35 back.

'Oh, Tom. You didn't make any marks.'

'Becky, I was such a fool. I never thought we might want to come back. No, I can't find the way. It's all mixed up.'

'Tom, Tom, we're lost, we're lost. We never, never can get out of this awful place. Oh, why did we ever leave the others?'

She sat down and began to cry. Tom sat beside her and put his arms round her. He blamed himself for getting her lost in this terrible place. She said he wasn't to talk like that. It wasn't all his fault. After a while they went on again. Tom took Becky's candle and blew it out, saying that they must save all the light they had. She knew he had a whole candle, and some pieces in his pocket. Even so, he must save them for later.

It's hopeless

After walking on for a very long way, Becky was too tired to continue. She sat down and Tom rested with her. They talked about home, and comfortable beds, and the light outside. Becky cried again, and Tom tried to comfort her, but it was no use. At last she fell asleep. Tom was glad. She looked very peaceful, and had a smile on her lips as if she was having a lovely dream. When she woke up, they agreed to go on trying to find their way out. They couldn't tell how long they had been in the cave, but it seemed like days and weeks. It was clearly not that long, for they still had their candles left.

A long time after this, Tom said they must go softly and listen for running water. They must find a stream. They found one soon, and Tom said it was time to rest again. Both were very tired, but Becky said she thought she could go on for a little more. She was surprised when Tom said no. She could not understand it.

They sat down, and Tom fastened his candle to the wall
in front of them with some mud. Nothing was said for
some time, then Becky broke the silence.

'Tom, I am so hungry.'

Tom took something out of his pocket.

'I saved a piece of cake from the picnic,' he said.

He divided the cake and they ate part of it. There
was plenty of water to drink. Becky said that they
should go on now, but Tom was silent. After a minute
or two he said, 'Becky, can you bear it if I tell you
something?'

Becky's face turned pale, but she said she thought
she could.

'Well, then, Becky, we must stay here, where there's
water to drink. That little piece is our last candle.'

Becky began to cry. At last she said, 'Tom.'

'Yes, Becky?'

'They'll miss us and hunt for us.'

'Yes they will. Of course they will.'

'Perhaps they're hunting for us now, Tom?'

'Well, perhaps they are. I hope they are.'

'When would they miss us, Tom?'

'When they get back to the boat, I think.'

'Tom, it might be dark, then. Would they notice we
hadn't come?'

'I don't know. But anyway, your mother would miss
you as soon as they got home.'

The frightened look on Becky's face made Tom
remember something. Becky was not expected home
that night. The children became silent and thoughtful.
Now they knew that Sunday morning might have
passed before Mrs Thatcher discovered that Becky was
not at Mrs Harper's. They fixed their eyes on the candle
and watched it melt slowly away. They watched as the
flame died. Then there was complete darkness.

Tom sees a light

Neither of them remembered falling asleep, but they must have done so. After what seemed a very long time they woke. Tom said he thought it might be Sunday now, even Monday. He tried to get Becky to talk, but she was too sad. Tom said that they must have been missed long ago, and people would be searching for them. The hours passed by. They felt hungry again, and ate the rest of the cake.

Then they heard a noise. It sounded like a far-off shout. At once Tom answered it, and leading Becky by the hand, started to feel his way down the passage towards it. He stopped to listen, and again they heard the sound, a little nearer now.

'It's them,' said Tom. 'They're coming. Come along, Becky, we're all right now.'

They could not hurry, because there were a lot of holes in the floor of the passage. Some might be shallow, and some could be deep. At last they came to one and had to stop. It might be three feet deep, or it might be a hundred feet, there was no way of telling. Tom lay on the floor and reached as far down as he could. There was no bottom. They must stay there and wait until the searchers came. They listened. The noises were going away from them now. A minute or two more, and they had gone altogether.

Tom shouted until his throat was sore, but it was no use. They felt their way very carefully back to the spring. They slept again and woke very hungry and frightened. Tom believed it must be Tuesday by this time.

Now he had a new idea. There were some side passages near where they were sitting. It would be better to explore some of them, than to sit doing

nothing. He took a kite-string out of his pocket, and
tied it to a piece of rock. He and Becky started out,
Tom in the lead, feeling his way along. After twenty
steps, the passage ended in dark space. They could go
no further. Tom got down on his knees and felt below,
and then as far round the corner as his arm would go.
He tried hard to stretch even more to the right.
Just then there was light. Only twenty yards away, a
human hand, holding a candle appeared from behind
a large rock. Tom gave a loud shout, and immediately
that hand was followed by a body. And the body it
belonged to was Injun Joe's. Tom could not move. He
was very glad to see Injun Joe turn quickly and step
back out of sight.
Then everything
was dark again.

He was surprised that Joe had not known him and come over and killed him for speaking out in court. But the cave must have changed the sound of his voice. He was careful not to tell Becky what he had seen. He told her he had only shouted 'for luck'. They went back to the spring again.

There was another awful wait, and another long sleep. The children woke in pain, because they were so hungry. Tom believed it must be Wednesday or Thursday, or even Friday or Saturday, now, and that the search had finished. He decided to explore another passage. Anything was better than waiting there — even meeting Injun Joe. But Becky was very weak. She said she would wait, now, where she was and die. It would not be long. She told Tom to go with the kite-string and explore, if he wanted to. But she asked him to keep coming back to speak to her. And she made him promise that when the awful time came, he would stay by her and hold her hand until it was all over. Tom kissed her, feeling very sad, and said he was sure he would find a way out of the cave. Then, holding the kite-string, he felt his way down one of the passages on his hands and knees. He was so hungry that he felt sick. He, too, had almost given up hope.

HAPPY ENDINGS

Tom finds the way out

Tuesday afternoon came and went. The village of St Petersburg was a very sad place. The children had not been found. Prayers had been said for them, but
5 still no good news came from the cave. Most of the men had given up the search, saying it was clear that the children could never be found. Mrs Thatcher was very ill. People said it was heart-breaking to hear her call her child, and raise her head and listen, then lay
10 down again with a soft cry. Aunt Polly's grey hair had grown almost white. The village went sadly to bed on Tuesday night.

In the middle of the night, the church bells began to ring. In a few minutes the streets were full of half-
15 dressed people, who shouted, 'Come out! Come out! They're found! They're found!' Everybody moved towards the river, to meet the children. They came, riding in an open waggon, pulled by a crowd of joyful men.
20 Nobody went to bed again. It was the greatest night the little village had ever seen. People went to Judge Thatcher's house
25 to hug the saved ones and squeeze Mrs Thatcher's hand.

Aunt Polly was very, very happy. Mrs Thatcher sent a message to her husband, who was still up at the cave searching for the children.

Tom sat with an eager audience around him, and told his story. He finished by describing how he had left 5 Becky and gone on his own to explore. He had tried two passages as far as his kite-string would reach, and then a third. He was about to turn back, when he saw, far away, something that looked like daylight. He had dropped the line and felt his way towards it. He pushed 10 his head and shoulders through a small hole and saw the great River Mississippi rolling by. If it had happened in the night, he wouldn't have noticed that tiny bit of daylight, and would not have explored that passage any more! 15

He told them how he had gone back to Becky to let her know the good news. She had told him not to worry her, for she was tired and very weak. He had made her believe him, and she had nearly died for joy when she saw the daylight. He had pushed his way out of the 20 hole, then helped her out. They had sat, crying with happiness, until some men came along in a boat. Tom had shouted to them and told them what had happened. They didn't believe his story at first. 'You are five miles down the river from where the cave 25 is!' they said. But they took the children into the boat, rowed to a house, gave them supper, made them rest until it was dark, and then brought them home.

It was two days before Tom was allowed out of bed. He went out for a while on Friday and was completely 30 well on Saturday, but Becky did not leave her room until Sunday. The poor child looked as if she had had a terrible illness, she was so thin.

Tom heard that Huck was sick. He went to the Welshman's to see him on Friday, but he was told to 35 go away. He couldn't see him on Saturday or Sunday, either, but on Monday he was let in. He had to promise, however, that he would not make Huck excited. The Widow Douglas stayed in the room to see that he obeyed. At home, Tom heard that the ragged man's body had been found in the river near the ferry landing. He had drowned while trying to escape.

About two weeks after Tom's adventure in the cave, he set off to visit Huck. Huck was now strong enough to hear exciting talk, and Tom had some that would interest him. Judge Thatcher's house was on Tom's way, and he stopped to see Becky. The Judge and some friends were there, and someone asked him, as a joke, if he would like to visit the cave again. Tom said yes, he thought he wouldn't mind it.

The Judge said, 'Well, there are others like you, Tom. But we have taken care of that. Nobody will get lost in that cave any more.'

'Why?'

'Because I had its big door covered with a sheet of iron and shut tight two weeks ago. I had three locks put on it. And I've got the keys.'

Tom turned as white as a sheet.

'What's the matter, boy? Here, run, somebody. Bring a glass of water.'

The water was brought and thrown into Tom's face.

'Ah, now you're better. What was the matter with you, Tom?'

'Oh, Judge, Injun Joe's in the cave.'

The death of Injun Joe

In a few minutes the news had spread, and men were once more on their way to McDougal's cave. The ferry-boat, well filled with passengers, followed the small

boats up the river. Tom Sawyer was in the same boat
as Judge Thatcher. When the cave door was opened, a
sad scene met their eyes. Injun Joe lay stretched upon
the ground, dead. His face was close to a small hole in
the door, as if he had been trying to look outside. Tom   5
felt sorry for the man, for he knew how he must have
felt. It had almost happened to him.

Injun Joe's knife lay close by. Its blade was broken
into two pieces. Marks on the door showed where he
had tried to cut his way out of the cave. But it had been   10
hopeless. Usually one could find pieces of candle in
the cave entrance, left by visitors. But there were none,
now. The prisoner had searched them out and eaten
them. He had also managed to catch a few bats, and
these, also, he had eaten, leaving only the hardest   15
bones. The poor man had died of hunger.

Injun Joe was buried near the mouth of the cave.
People came in boats and waggons from the
village, and from all the farms and
villages around. They brought food
with them. Later they said that
they had had almost as good a
time at Indian Joe's funeral as
they would have done if he
had been tried and hanged.

The morning after the
funeral, Tom took Huck to
a quiet place to have an
important talk. He had not
yet heard of the part Huck
had played in the adventure
on Cardiff Hill. He had only
heard the story from the
Welshman. Now Huck told
Tom the truth about that night,

and how he had seen the two men carrying the box away.

'And now we've lost it,' he said sadly.

'No we haven't,' said Tom excitedly, 'it's in the cave.'

'Say that again,' said Huck.

'The money's in the cave.'

'Are you joking, Tom?'

'No, Huck. Will you go there with me and get the money out?'

'You know I will, if it's where we can go safely and not get lost.'

'Huck, we can do it without any trouble at all.'

'All right. But what makes you so sure the money's in the cave?'

'Huck, you just wait till we get in there. If we don't find it, I'll agree to give you my kite and everything else I've got in the world.'

'All right. When do we go?'

'Right now, if you like. Are you strong enough?'

'Is it far in the cave? I've been out of bed for three or four days now, but I can't walk more than a mile, Tom.'

'It's about five miles the way anybody else would go, Huck. But there's a much shorter way that only I know about. I'll take you there in a boat.'

'Let's start right now, Tom.'

'We'll need to get some things first,' said Tom. 'We want some bread and some meat, some small bags and two or three kite-strings. And we need some matches. I wish I'd had some of those when I was in there before.'

Under the cross

It was early afternoon when the boys took a boat, and sailed off down the river. When they were several miles from the place where the cave entrance was, Tom said, 'We must go on shore here.'

They landed.

'Now, Huck, from where we're standing you could touch the hole I got out of. See if you can find it.'

Huck searched all around but found nothing. Tom proudly marched to a thick bush and said, 'Here you are. Look at it, Huck. Isn't it well hidden?'

Huck had to agree. The boys entered the hole, Tom in the lead. They made their way to the end of the passage, then tied their kite-strings to a rock and moved on. A few steps brought them to the stream, and Tom felt a shiver go all through him. He showed Huck where his last candle had burned, while he and Becky watched it go out.

They went on, and soon entered Tom's other passage which they followed until they came to the end.

'Now I'll show you something,' whispered Tom. He held his candle up and said, 'Look as far round the corner as you can. Do you see that? There, on the big rock, done with candle smoke.'

'Tom, it's a *cross*.'

'"*Under the cross*" hey? That's where Injun Joe meant. And that's where I saw Injun Joe hold up a candle.'

Huck stared at the sign for a while, and then said, 'Tom, let's get out of here.' He sounded frightened.

'What? And leave the treasure?'

'Yes, leave it, Tom. Injun Joe's ghost is round about there, I'm certain.'

'No it's not, Huck. It would haunt the place where he died, away at the cave mouth, and that's five miles from here.'

'No, Tom, it wouldn't. It would stay around the money. I know all about the ways of ghosts, and so do you.'

Tom began to think that Huck was right. But soon he had an idea.

'We're being silly, Huck. Injun Joe's ghost isn't going to come around where there's a cross.'

'I didn't think of that. But you're right. It's lucky for us that cross is there. Let's go down and hunt for the box.'

Tom went first and Huck followed. There were four passages close by the great rock. The boys explored three of them but found nothing. In one of them they found an old blanket, a belt, some small pieces of bacon and the bones of two or three chickens. But there was no treasure box.

'He said under the cross,' said Tom. 'Well this is nearest to being under the cross. It can't be under the rock itself.' They searched everywhere once more, and then sat down. Then Tom noticed something.

'Look here, Huck. There are footprints and candle wax on the ground on one side of this rock, but not on the other side. Now what's that for? I think the money is under the rock. I'm going to dig.'

'That's not a bad idea, Tom,' said Huck.

Tom took a knife from his pocket and began to dig. He had only gone down four inches when his knife struck wood.

'Hey, Huck. Did you hear that?'

'We're rich, Tom.'

Huck began to dig and scratch now. Some pieces of wood were soon uncovered and taken out. They had hidden the entrance to a small passage. Tom got into this and held his candle as far under the rock as he could, but said he could not see to the end. He bent down and pushed himself forward. Huck followed him in. The narrow passage went first to the right, and then to the left. Tom turned a corner and stopped.

'My goodness, Huck, look here.'

There was the treasure box. Beside it stood an empty powder barrel, two guns, some old shoes and some other rubbish.

'Got it at last,' said Huck, putting his hand into the box and pulling out some of the coins. 'We're rich, Tom.'

'Huck, I always knew we'd get it. It's just too good to believe. Let's not wait around here, let's take it out. Let me see if I can lift the box.'

It weighed about ten pounds. Tom could just lift it, but he couldn't carry it far.

'I thought so,' he said. 'They carried it as if it was very heavy, that day at the haunted house. I noticed that. I was right to think of bringing those small bags with us.'

The money was soon in the bags, and the boys took it up to the rock with the cross.

'Now let's fetch the guns and things,' said Huck.

'No, Huck, leave them there. We can come back some time and use them when we play at being pirates. Come along now, we've been here a long time. It's getting late, and I'm hungry, too. We'll have something to eat in the boat.'

They carried the bags back to the boat and pushed it into the water. The sun was already going down. By the time they landed near the village it was quite dark.

A home for Huck

The finding of that money completely changed the lives of Tom Sawyer and Huck Finn. The money was counted. They had found almost twelve thousand dollars. It was put into the bank where it would be safe and grow.

There was enough for each boy to have a dollar every day in the year for the next twenty years. A dollar a day, in those days, was plenty of money. It was enough to buy food and clothes for a boy, and send him to school.

The old Welshman told Widow Douglas about Huck and how he had help to save her from Injun Joe. Widow Douglas thanked Huck for what he had done. She said that from then on he must live with her. She wanted to give him a proper home, and send him to school.

At first Huck did not like this at all. He ran away, and went back to wearing ragged clothes and living in an old barrel. But Tom found him. Tom said he was going to start a gang of robbers. Huck wanted to join, but Tom wouldn't let him. Robbers, said Tom, were gentlemen, and Tom Sawyer's gang wouldn't have any low people in it — not people who dressed in rags and slept in barrels. Huck thought about it for a while and then decided to go back to Widow Douglas.

'If I become a really good robber, Tom,' he said, 'I know she'll be glad she let me live with her.'

QUESTIONS AND ACTIVITIES

CHAPTER 1

Choose the right words to say what the chapter is about.

Tom made Ben Rogers and the other boys think that
(1) **mending/painting** Aunty Polly's fence was not work. He
said that (2) **many/very few** boys could paint the fence the way
it had to be done. He said he was the only one who could do it
the (3) **right/wrong** way. Then all the boys wanted see if they
could (4) **go swimming/paint the fence**. They gave Tom
things so that he (5) **would not/would** let them help him.

CHAPTER 2

Put the sentences in the right order, to say what happened.

1   Then the dog sat down on the beetle.
2   A little dog began to play with the beetle.
3   Tom took a large black beetle to church.
4   The beetle pinched the dog and held on to him.
5   The beetle was thrown onto the floor.
6   The dog ran up and down the church yelping noisily.
7   Tom shook his hand.
8   The beetle pinched Tom's finger.

CHAPTER 3

*Some of these statements are true, but others are false. Which
are the true ones?*

1   Tom and Huck saw Potter attack the doctor.
2   They saw the doctor hit Potter.
3   Then they saw Injun Joe attack Potter with the doctor's knife.
4   The boys knew that Injun Joe had killed Potter.
5   They knew that Potter was unconscious at the time.

CHAPTER 4

Put the paragraphs in the right order to say what the story is about.

1 Tom did not answer. He did not want anyone to know about the awful secret. He did not want them to know he had seen Injun Joe kill Dr Robinson.

2 After that Tom tied a bandage round his head when he went to bed. He thought that would stop him talking.

3 Sid said Tom talked in his sleep so much he kept him awake. He told Aunt Polly that Tom talked about blood and telling someone something.

4 Then Aunty Polly said it was probably the murder that was giving Tom bad dreams. She said she dreamed about it nearly every night herself.

5 Aunt Polly said she thought this was a bad sign. She asked Tom what he was worried about.

CHAPTER 5

Put the beginnings of these sentences with the right endings.

1 The men on the ferry fired the gun ...

(a) ... because he wanted to see his mother.

2 The boys had a wonderful feeling ...

(b) ... because he was feeling lonely.

3 Tom's blood ran cold ...

(c) ... to make bodies rise to the top of the water.

4 Joe was nearly in tears ...

(d) ... because they liked Tom's plan.

5 Huck wanted to go back ...

(e) ... because he heard people talking about his funeral.

6 Huck and Joe decided to stay ...

(f) ... because they knew people were missing them.

CHAPTER 6

Fill the gaps by using each of these words once to say what the story is about: **stayed, stood, jumped, gave, told, kill, went, found.**

Tom and Huck thought if Injun Joe (1) ____ out they had seen the murder, he would (2) ____ them.

But they felt sorry for Muff Potter. They (3) ____ to the little prison and (4) ____ Muff Potter some tobacco and matches.

Then Tom (5) ____ out very late one night. He went to the lawyer and (6) ____ him the whole story. On the last day of the trial Tom (7) ____ in front of the people and told the truth. But Injun Joe (8) ____ through a window and got away.

CHAPTER 7

There is something wrong in the underlined part of all these sentences: correct them so they say what happened.

1 <u>Tom and Joe went to the haunted house</u> to look for treasure.
2 <u>When they were downstairs</u> two people came into the house.
3 <u>It was the blind and deaf Spaniard,</u> and another man.
4 The Spaniard <u>was really Muff Potter.</u>
5 The two men had hidden <u>some silver underneath the wooden floor</u>.
6 <u>They found some jewels</u> when they were digging for their silver.

CHAPTER 8

Put the words in each sentence in the right order.

1 An hour before midnight the	[crept] [inn] [towards] [boys] [the].
2 Tom tried to open the	[room] [number] [door] [two] [of].
3 Then Tom found that	[not] [the] [locked] [was] [door].

4 Tom went into the room   [Joe's] [on] [stepped] [hand]
and almost   [Injun].
5 Tom ran away   [so] [he] [was] [because]
                                 [frightened].

CHAPTER 9

*Copy the table and write the answers in their correct places.
Choose from:* **followed, Welshman, Widow, found, bury,
Huck, hidden, face, quarry, river, Douglas.** *The name of
a place in the story will appear in the centre of the table.*

(1) ____ thought the two men were going to (2) ____ the box
somewhere, so he (3) ____ them. The men went along the
(4) ____ road and then turned left up another street. Then they
went straight on until they came to a path.

They went up the path, past the (5) ____'s house. Huck thought
they must be going to the (6) ____ to bury the box there. The
men did not stop, but went on until they came to a path (7) ____
between tall bushes.

Huck thought he had lost the men. Then he (8) ____ them, close
to the gate which led to (9) ____ (10) ____'s place. He heard
them say they were going to hurt the poor woman. Injun Joe
wanted to cut her (11) ____.

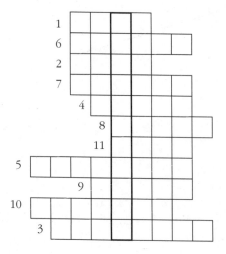

CHAPTER 10

Which of these names go in the gaps? You will need to use some names more than once: **Mrs Harper, Aunt Polly, Mrs Thatcher, Joe, Tom.**

(1) ____ thought Tom had stayed with (2) ____ or Mrs Thatcher. She thought (3) ____ had not come to church because he was afraid after staying out all night. But Mrs Harper said (4) ____ had not stayed with her or (5) ____. (6) ____ asked (7) ____ if he had seen Tom that morning. (8) ____ said he had not seen him. Then everyone started to look worried.

CHAPTER 11

Choose the right words to say what happens.

Tom said that they must listen for (1) **the rain/running water/ a well**. They must find a stream. After a while they found one, and Tom told Becky that they must (2) **rest/drink/wash there**. When Becky said she thought she could go on for a little more, Tom said they must (3) **hurry to the cave entrance/go to sleep/stay by the stream**.

Becky said she was (4) **thirsty/happy/hungry**. Tom took something out of his pocket. It was a piece of (5) **cake/bread/ fruit** that he had saved from the picnic. Tom divided the food and they ate (6) **all/none/part of it**.

CHAPTER 12

The letters in these words are all mixed up. What should they be? (The first one is 'candle'.)

Tom took Huck to where someone had drawn a cross in (1) **lanced** smoke on a big rock. He thought that must be where Injun Joe had (2) **ubdier** his treasure. Then Tom saw some (3) **storpofint** on the ground. He thought the (4) **yemno** must be under the rock. He began to dig. He found the (5) **rectenna** to a small passage. Tom got into the passage and pushed himself (6) **rafdowr**. The passage went first to the right, then to the left. When Tom turned a corner he saw the (7) **aresrute** box.

GRADE 1

Alice's [Adventures in]
Wonderland
Lewis Carroll

The Call of the Wild [and]
Other Stories
Jack London

Emma
Jane Austen

Jane Eyre
Charlotte Brontë

Little Women
Louisa M. Alcott

**The Lost Umbrella of Kim
Chu**
Eleanor Estes

**Tales From the Arabian
Nights**
Edited by David Foulds

Treasure Island
Robert Louis Stevenson

Ch[...]

**The Ta[...]
Stories**
David McRobbie

Through the Looking [Glass]
Lewis Carroll

**The Stone Junk and Other
Stories**
D.H. Howe

GRADE 2

**The Adventures of Sherlock
Holmes**
Sir Arthur Conan Doyle

A Christmas Carol
Charles Dickens

**The Dagger and Wings and
Other Father Brown Stories**
G.K. Chesterton

**The Flying Heads and Other
Strange Stories**
Edited by David Foulds

**The Golden Touch and
Other Stories**
Edited by David Foulds

**Gulliver's Travels —
A Voyage to Lilliput**
Jonathan Swift

GRADE 3

**The Adventures of Tom
Sawyer**
Mark Twain

**Around the World in Eighty
Days**
Jules Verne

**The Canterville Ghost and
Other Stories**
Oscar Wilde

David Copperfield
Charles Dickens

Fog and Other Stories
Bill Lowe

**Further Adventures of
Sherlock Holmes**
Sir Arthur Conan Doyle

GRA...

**Alice's
Won...**
Lewis Carroll

**The Call of the Wild and
Other Stories**
Jack London

Emma
Jane Austen

Jane Eyre
Charlotte Brontë

Little Women
Louisa M. Alcott

**The Lost Umbrella of Kim
Chu**
Eleanor Estes

**Tales From the Arabian
Nights**
Edited by David Foulds

Treasure Island
Robert Louis Stevenson

DA... ...yard Kipling

**Life Without Katy and Other
Stories**
O. Henry

Lord Jim
Joseph Conrad

**A Midsummer Night's Dream
and Other Stories from
Shakespeare's Plays**
Edited by David Foulds

Oliver Twist
Charles Dickens

**The Talking Tree and Other
Stories**
David McRobbie

Through the Looking Glass
Lewis Carroll

**The Stone Junk and Other
Stories**
D.H. Howe

GRADE 2

**The Adventures of Sherlock
Holmes**
Sir Arthur Conan Doyle

A Christmas Carol
Charles Dickens

**The Dagger and Wings and
Other Father Brown Stories**
G.K. Chesterton

**The Flying Heads and Other
Strange Stories**
Edited by David Foulds

**The Golden Touch and
Other Stories**
Edited by David Foulds

**Gulliver's Travels —
A Voyage to Lilliput**
Jonathan Swift

GRADE 3

**The Adventures of Tom
Sawyer**
Mark Twain

**Around the World in Eighty
Days**
Jules Verne

**The Canterville Ghost and
Other Stories**
Oscar Wilde

David Copperfield
Charles Dickens

Fog and Other Stories
Bill Lowe

**Further Adventures of
Sherlock Holmes**
Sir Arthur Conan Doyle

CHAPTER 10

Which of these names go in the gaps? You will need to use some names more than once: **Mrs Harper, Aunt Polly, Mrs Thatcher, Joe, Tom.**

(1) ____ thought Tom had stayed with (2) ____ or Mrs Thatcher. She thought (3) ____ had not come to church because he was afraid after staying out all night. But Mrs Harper said (4) ____ had not stayed with her or (5) ____. (6) ____ asked (7) ____ if he had seen Tom that morning. (8) ____ said he had not seen him. Then everyone started to look worried.

CHAPTER 11

Choose the right words to say what happens.

Tom said that they must listen for (1) **the rain/running water/ a well**. They must find a stream. After a while they found one, and Tom told Becky that they must (2) **rest/drink/wash there**. When Becky said she thought she could go on for a little more, Tom said they must (3) **hurry to the cave entrance/go to sleep/stay by the stream**.

Becky said she was (4) **thirsty/happy/hungry**. Tom took something out of his pocket. It was a piece of (5) **cake/bread/ fruit** that he had saved from the picnic. Tom divided the food and they ate (6) **all/none/part of it**.

CHAPTER 12

The letters in these words are all mixed up. What should they be? (The first one is 'candle'.)

Tom took Huck to where someone had drawn a cross in (1) **lanced** smoke on a big rock. He thought that must be where Injun Joe had (2) **ubdier** his treasure. Then Tom saw some (3) **storpofint** on the ground. He thought the (4) **yemno** must be under the rock. He began to dig. He found the (5) **rectenna** to a small passage. Tom got into the passage and pushed himself (6) **rafdowr**. The passage went first to the right, then to the left. When Tom turned a corner he saw the (7) **aresrute** box.